CW00972733

www.jessicaamesauthor.com

Blackjack is a work of fiction. Names, places, characters, and incidents are a product of the author's imagination and are fictitious. Any resemblance to actual persons living or dead, events, or establishments is solely coincidental.

Editor – Farrant Editing

Proofreader – Gem's Precise Proofreads

Cover Model – Matthew Hosea

Cover Designer – Reggie Deanching

Alpha Readers – Jayne Ruston, Clara Martinez Turco

Beta Readers – Allisyn Pentleton, Lynne Garlick, Pat Labrie

Please note: this book contains material aimed at an adult audience, including sex, violence, and bad language.

AUTHOR'S NOTE

This book contains upsetting themes. For a full list of these themes visit:

https://www.jessicaamesauthor.com/jessicaamestwcw

This book is set in the United Kingdom. Some spellings may differ.

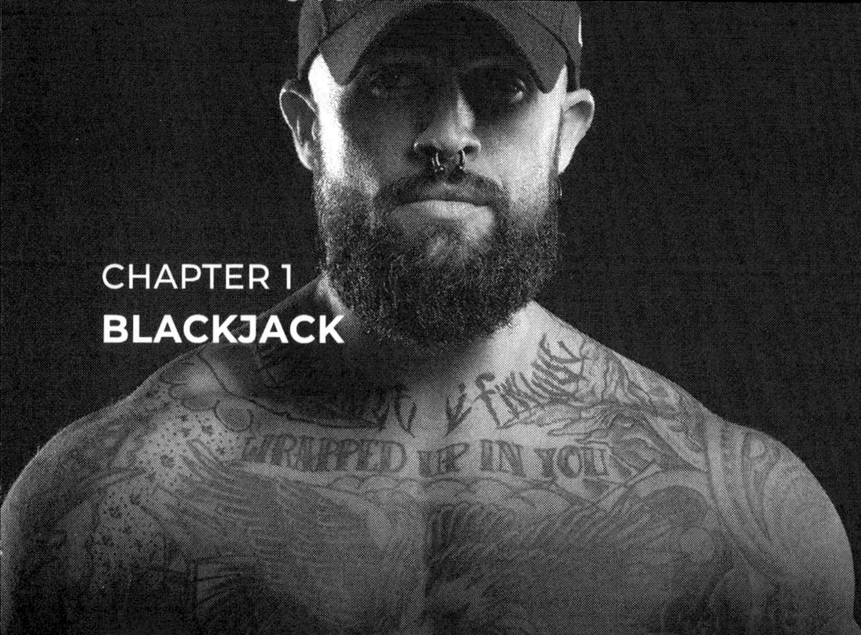

CHAPTER 1
BLACKJACK

There's nothing I love more than playing cards. Blackjack is what I love, but I like to dabble in Poker. Texas Hold 'em is my game of choice, but I do play the occasional hand of Omaha when I need the change.

For as long as I can remember, I've played these games. My grandfather taught me when I used to visit him as a kid. He would sit for hours, dealing cards and showing me all the tricks he knew. I fucking loved spending that time with him. It didn't occur to me until I was older that he was a card shark. I later found out that everything my grandfather owned was bought because of cards.

One of the games I loved more than all the others was blackjack. I learnt early on how to count the cards in a way that I could guess with almost certainty what was coming next—a high or low card. It was easy as fuck to track, and I was good at it. That love of the game was how I got my road name when I joined the Sons' London chapter. Blackjack. I wore that name like fucking armour, like all my brothers did. Road names were sacred.

Before we moved to Manchester and established the club here, I used to go to some of the biggest casinos in London. Over the years, I won enough to live comfortably for the rest of my fucking life. I could have left the club, could have left everything behind and retired, but it was never about the money. I didn't give a fuck about how much I had in my accounts or how many bikes I owned. I didn't give a fuck about the houses I could buy either.

It was the thrill of the game that got me, and the reminder of the man who created Blackjack—my grandfather. Fuck, I miss that old bastard every day.

Because of him, I lived and breathed the adrenaline rush that came with beating cocky arseholes at the table. I loved how people underestimated me when they saw my tattoos covering my body. I loved proving them wrong.

As I walk through the casino, members of staff greet me with smiles and nods. I come here whenever I can. It's the only way I know to take the edge off after a shitty day, and this day—this week, in fact—has been hard. We've been doing a lot of runs between us and our Birmingham chapter, moving supplies of drugs and guns ready for sale. It was big business for us, and it was also dangerous. It could land any one of us in jail for a long fucking time. It was how we made money for the club. The guns came to us from our Tennessee brothers. We sold those weapons to lower level gangs and clubs.

I've been visiting this casino for years. It's less than a mile from the clubhouse and they know I'm club. Though

I'm not allowed to wear my kutte inside the building. No colours, no gang affiliations—it was about the game inside these walls. I hate taking my kutte off. I hate leaving it in my flat. I feel fucking naked without it on my back, but it's the price I have to pay to play.

Instead of my jeans and a hoodie, I'm wearing a button-up shirt and dark wash jeans. It is as close to a suit as I can manage.

I take my seat at the blackjack table and rub my hands together as the dealer reaches into the shoe and takes the deck from it. Three suited fuckers are sitting at the table, eyeing me as I get comfortable. I can feel the judgement behind their stares. I know they have underestimated me instantly.

Good.

I'll enjoy taking their fucking money.

For the next few hours, I get lost in the game, letting all the tension drain from my body as I bet more and more money. I don't know how much I've won so far, but it's over a grand at least.

After a while, I move to the poker table, needing a change of scenery. I'm not as good at poker as I am blackjack, but that just adds to the thrill when I win.

The game is just coming to a close. A new deal will be made, and I can join the pool then. As I wait, I'm aware of someone sliding onto the chair next to me.

I twist as a petite redhead, with a rack that makes my cock harden, sits. She's fucking stunning. Her dark green dress clings to her body something fierce, hugging her curves and thighs. It should be illegal to look that good.

Her wavy hair falls down her back and her makeup is thick, dark and stunning. She catches my gaze, and her mouth pulls into a smile that goes straight to my fucking dick.

Holy shit.

I want her.

Images of her bent over the table while I pound into her cunt fill my head.

The dealer says something to me, but I don't pull my attention back to the table. Instead, I watch as she picks up a Champagne flute and takes a drink. The way her throat moves as she sips, her lips against the glass…

Fuck.

"Are you in?" the dealer repeats.

"I'm in," she says.

Her words surprise me. She doesn't look like a serious player—then again, neither do I. People see my appearance and make assumptions. I don't think that's what I'm doing with her. I think she's clueless about poker, or any other card game in this room.

In truth, I don't give a fuck about her skills. I'm focused on the way she smells. Her perfume fills my nose, and I resist the urge to lean in and run my nose along her neck.

I toss a hundred-pound betting chip into the betting box and she follows my lead.

"I don't have a clue what I'm doing," she admits as the dealer starts to deal the cards in front of each player.

I smirk. I was right.

"First time in a casino or first time playing poker?"

Her cheeks pink up. My eyes drop to her fucking gorgeous mouth. She's wearing bright red lipstick that I want to see around the head of my cock.

"Both." Her nose wrinkles. "Is it that obvious?"

"Just a little," I laugh. "You've got rookie written all over you."

"I've seen it played, know how it works in theory, but I've never played it with anyone other than my brother."

"So, you pick a casino filled with professional fucking card players as your first outing?"

She laughs. "I can see why you'd think that's crazy. I figured it was a good plan to leap in at the deep end. Sink or swim, right?"

"Everyone has to learn," I say. "But your first mistake was sitting here. You should have picked another table."

Her brows cock. "Why's that?"

"Because I'm going to clean up here."

She rolls her eyes. "I admire your bravado."

"Ain't bravado. I'm the best fucking player in this room." Poker ain't my first love, but I can play it, and well.

She studies me for a moment. "Also the most modest."

I smirk. The banter feels good, natural. It feels like I've known her for years, not minutes. The chemistry between us crackles. I've never had this with any woman before. The connection is soul deep. "Truth is the truth."

"Your accent isn't local," she says as the dealer deals the cards.

"I'm from London, but I've been here for a few years now. What about you?"

"Born and raised in Salford."

Salford is west of Ancoats, less than a fifteen-minute drive. We have a couple of allies in that area.

"You sure you want to do this?" I ask her, even though it's too late for her to back out. The bet has been placed. She has to play the game.

She nods and blows out a breath, her eyes twinkling with excitement. "When in Rome, right?"

"Babe, I'm just going to take your money."

She juts her chin out like a petulant kid. "I might get lucky."

Doubtful, but I like her optimism. The cards are dealt. I watch her as she tries to play. She's fucking adorable.

It's clear she has no fucking idea what she's doing. My initial hand is good, a lucky draw. Three of a kind. If I can get lucky and make it four of a kind, I should win the round, providing no one else has a straight flush.

From the way her eyes dart around, I surmise her hand is not good. Even so, she meets the bets that are placed by the other players. I find myself watching her, not the other players. I don't give a shit if I lose this game; I can't take my fucking eyes off her.

There's something about that innocence in her that makes me intrigued. I want to know more about her. I'm used to being around harder women. The club bunnies and hangarounds that come through the club aren't there because they have a good fucking life. Red seems… different.

The game comes to a conclusion, and though I didn't manage to find my fourth card, I beat everyone on the table, including Red. She had the worst hand I've ever seen.

"I thought beginners were supposed to have luck," she pouts as the dealer places the chips I won in my box.

I grab her hand and pull her up from the table.

"What are you doing?" she asks, curious rather than freaked at being manhandled by a huge, hulking man.

"I'm saving you from more defeat. Come and have a drink with me," I say to her.

"Drinking I can do far better than cards."

I need to touch her. It's overwhelming. I press my hand to the small of her back, steering her towards the bar. She feels fucking good against my palm. My cock is fucking awake and ready for action. I want her. Every cell in my body wants her.

And not just because she's fucking beautiful, which she is, but because I can sense a vulnerability in her. Her uncertainty at the poker table told me she doesn't belong here, not really. I want to protect her from losing all her money—though why I care, I don't know.

She goes to a table near to the floor so we can see over the tables, watch the games as they're played. I slip into the seat opposite her. I want to look into her eyes when I talk to her. She's got gorgeous green irises that are incandescent.

"Why'd you come to a casino if you can't play cards?" I ask.

Red shifts her shoulders. "Why does anyone gamble?"

To win money. I wonder what she wants money for. "You'd be better playing the lottery."

She snorts. "Less chance of winning though. At least here I'm in with a shot of coming home with something."

"I don't know. You were pretty bad back there."

"What a compliment."

"What's your name?"

"What's yours?" she fires back on a smile.

"Matt." I give her my real name. I'm not sure why I do that either. I don't give my name out to anyone. I follow up with, "But my club brothers call me Blackjack."

"Because... you're good at blackjack?" She laughs as the realisation dawns on her face. "If I'd known that, I wouldn't have tried to play you."

"If we were playing blackjack at that table, I'd have beaten you sooner. I ain't as good at poker, but cards are my life, babe. Been playing them since I was a kid. Most of the players in this room are fucking experts at cards." It isn't a lie. There's a couple of bachelor parties in, having a laugh, but the majority of players come to win serious cash or because they're addicted to the tables.

"I must have seemed crazy to you then." She buries her face in her hands to hide her mortification.

"I didn't think you were crazy. Maybe naive, but not crazy."

"That's not an improvement." She stares at me a beat. "You said club brothers. Are you in some sort of card club?"

I laugh. "No, babe. I'm Vice President of the Untamed Sons Motorcycle Club."

A hint of fear flashes through her eyes. It's something I'm used to seeing when our name is mentioned. Our club has a reputation—the Manchester chapter especially. We'd spilt a ton of blood to carve out our territory. Joe Public knew it because the papers and local media reported every time we took a fucking shit. Most people are scared of our name, of our affiliations, of what we represent.

I reach out and tuck her hair behind her ear, needing to touch her somehow. Needing to reassure her that I may be a monster, but she's safe with me.

"Ain't nothing to be scared of," I tell her. "I won't hurt you. I won't do anything you don't want me to, but I'd really like to fuck you."

Her eyes heat at my words as she pulls her bottom lip between her teeth.

She dips her head, a little coy. I like that shit too.

"What would you say if I told you the real reason I'm here is because I'm tired of picking up little boys pretending to be men in clubs and bars."

I grin. "Then let me show you what you're missing."

I take her hand and pull her up from the table. She's not as brazen as she's putting on. I can feel her slight tremble as I head towards the front desk of the casino. I like that she's nervous. It means she doesn't make a habit of picking up random men.

She says nothing as I book a room at the front desk of the casino. I don't live far away, but I don't make a habit of taking strangers back to my place. My flat is my sanctuary; a room in the casino keeps things neutral.

Once I have the keys from the desk clerk, I lead Red over to the lifts and push the button to call it.

"You want to walk away, now is the time," I say, glancing at her as we wait for the lift to come. I give her an out, something I would never give a club bunny, but she ain't like those bitches. I sure as fuck hope she won't take the out, but I know I need to give it.

To my relief, she shakes her head. "Why would I do that?"

I grin.

The doors open on a ping, and we step inside. It's just the two of us, so as soon as the doors slide shut behind us, I push Red against the wall of the lift. Her eyes are wide, but heated.

I don't waste any time. I dip my head low, and I devour her mouth, something I've wanted to do from the moment I laid eyes on her. Normally, I don't kiss, but I want to own her mouth in a way I've never thought about before. I want to own her. Dominate.

She isn't shy. She lets me inside, her tongue caressing along mine. Her hands run up my back as I reach under her dress so I can cup her between her legs. The gasp she makes goes straight to my cock.

Fuck, I can't wait to get her to the room and be inside her.

I settle for running my fingers over her underwear. She's wet. The material is soaked.

"Is all this for me, baby?" I ask her, speaking into her ear.

"Yes," she whimpers as I push her knickers aside and slide a finger into her waiting channel. "Matt..."

I like hearing my name on her lips. I especially like the

way she invokes it, almost as if she's praying. I add another finger, then I use both to fuck her against the wall of the lift. My digits hook into her pussy, seeking that spot inside her that I know will drive her wild.

She grips my wrist, whether to pull me free or push me deeper, I can't tell. I don't care either. I'm too focused on the way her eyes are squeezed shut as she tries to control her breathing.

Before she can go over the edge, the doors slide open on our floor. Reluctantly, I pull my fingers out of her and lift the juice covered tips to my mouth. Red watches as I suck them clean, her face flushing.

"That was…"

She breaks off, her breath tearing out of her.

"I want to get you in that room and take my time with you," I say.

Grabbing her hand as she straightens her dress with the other, I pull her out of the lift. The hallway is quiet. There is no noise coming from any of the rooms we pass. I'm not sure how much noise will be coming from our room in the next five seconds, but I hope they have good soundproofing. I'm going to make her fucking scream.

My cock is unbearably tight against my zip as I lead her to the room number on the room key and insert the card into the lock. The green light flashes, and I open the door.

I don't give a second glance to what the room looks like. As soon as Red is inside the room and the door is shut behind us, I push her against the wall again and clamp my mouth to hers.

Her arms wrap around my neck, pulling me closer as she kisses me back. My cock feels solid in my jeans, needing its release.

I shove her dress up to her hips and get on my knees in front of her. She looks fucking stunning; her lips swollen from my kisses; her hair mussed. Sliding her underwear down her legs, I get my first look at her pussy. She's bare, apart from a small patch of trimmed hair just above. I part her folds and press my face against her cunt. She smells divine. I dart my tongue out and find her clit, circling it.

She starts to shift slightly, but I hold her in place, my hands firmly attached to her hips as I eat her out.

"Matt..." she gasps my name again, followed by a spluttering, *"Fuck!"*

I lick and nip, using every trick I know to bring her to orgasm. She starts to writhe under my tongue, and her pants become more desperate.

"I'm going to... I'm going..."

She tips her head back against the wall as her orgasm rips through her. As it does, she grips my head, pulling me tighter against her. Her juices coat my beard and face, but I don't move to wipe either.

I peer up at her, enjoying her climax. I love the way she's wriggling and clamping her thighs together.

I need to fuck her, and I need to do it soon.

I stand and lift her off the ground. Her legs instinctively wrap around my back as I walk us over to the bed. She isn't heavy, and I like how her tits press against my chest as we lock mouths in the short intervening space between the door and the bed.

The sheets are pristine, white and neatly tucked around the mattress. I can't wait to fuck them up.

I lower her onto the bed and push her legs wide apart.

"Fuck," I murmur, running my thumb over my lips as I admire her spread for me. She looks like a sacrifice. Her dress is around her hips, allowing her to open her legs as wide as she needs to, and all I can see is her pretty, pink, glistening pussy.

"I want to fuck that pretty cunt of yours."

Her cheeks pink up at my words. "Do you always talk like that?"

"If you're looking for a Prince fucking Charming, babe, I ain't it."

"I never said I wanted a Prince Charming."

"What do you want then?"

"You."

It's all the invitation I need.

I toe off my boots, then I strip out of my shirt and jeans, tossing both garments onto the floor and leaving me just in my boxer briefs. The outline of my cock is an unmistakable presence, but it's not my dick that snares her attention. It's the rest of my body. My chest and arms are a canvas, covered in tattoos. My clothes hid most of it, so I understand her intrigue.

"That's so beautiful," she murmurs. "Do they all have a meaning behind them?" Her eyes roam over my bare chest, trying to take in every piece of art.

"Yeah, they do." I don't elaborate. I want to fuck her, not discuss my body.

"I've always wanted a tattoo, but I don't like needles. Did they hurt?"

"Babe, do you really want to talk about my fucking tatts?"

She meets my eyes, shaking her head. "I want you to fuck me."

"That, I can do."

I lean over the bed and pull the top of her dress down until it's gathered just below her bare tits. Fuck me. Her dusty pink nipples are hard as bullets, the creamy skin flawless. Latching onto one of the buds, I suck it into my mouth, plumping her tit as I do. Instantly, she moans and arches her back. Not all women like having their tits played with, but Red nearly comes off the bed as I swirl my tongue over hers.

"Fuck," she hisses out, forcing the word between clenched teeth.

Her breaths become more desperate, more needy, as I nip and suck her tits, moving between the right and left. Her hand drifts between us to her clit, and I feel her moving between our bodies.

Once I have her writhing beneath me, close to coming again, I stand from the bed and lower my underwear. My cock is hard as a rock as I fist it between my fingers, giving it a tug. My balls feel so tight they hurt a little. I need my release, and I need it fast.

I reach into my jeans pocket and pull out my wallet. There's a condom stuffed in the back of it. I pull it out and tear it open, carefully removing the condom. Pinching the top, I expertly roll it down my shaft, making sure it's in place. I don't want any fucking mini-Blackjack's running around.

When I'm sure it's in place, I move back to the bed. I pull her to the edge of the mattress until her arse is hanging over the edge, so I can pound into her easily. She peers up at me. She looks fucking sated and ready for what's coming next.

"What's your name?" I ask.

I don't expect her to answer. She dodged the question last time, so I'm surprised when she says, "Elyse."

Fucking beautiful name for a beautiful woman.

"I'm going to fuck you now, Elyse," I tell her.

A small smile plays over her lips. "Yes."

I keep my eyes locked on hers as I line up with her cunt. I don't look away as I slowly push inside her. Her wetness eases my passage, but she squeezes around my cock as I move deeper. It's like she's already trying to milk my dick. If she keeps this up, I'm not going to fucking last.

It takes a little to push through. She's tight and a little tense. I run my hand over her belly, trying to calm her. "Open up for me."

She widens her thighs and winces a little as my cock slides deeper. "You're big," she says.

I am. I'm six foot six and my cock is well in proportion to the rest of my body. I am a lot to take, which is why I move slowly, letting her stretch around me.

"Relax," I say in a soft voice.

I give her a moment to get used to my girth before I drag my cock out of her, to the tip. She groans, fisting the sheets.

"Okay?" I ask.

She nods. "Fuck me."

I smirk and begin to piston my hips. Every drag of my cock through her channel makes me see fucking stars.

She feels amazing. I angle my hips, rotating them as I fuck her, trying to push as deep as I can. Holding her hips in place, I pick up my pace, fucking her hard and fast.

This isn't like screwing a club bunny. Those bitches only want to get their claws in because they hope one of us will make them an old lady. Ain't happening. I know Levi from the London Chapter took on a bunny, but that ain't the fucking norm.

Elyse ain't looking for what she can get off me. She ain't making moves, hoping it will benefit her.

That's refreshing.

This is just pure and simple attraction.

I slam deeper and harder, pushing her up the mattress.

"Matt… more…" she pleads.

I deliver, finding a rhythm and pace that has her gasping with each pound of my hips. The way our eyes connect is like nothing I've ever experienced. I've never fucked where it meant something. Usually, I fuck to take the edge off. Already, this doesn't feel like that.

Her back suddenly arcs off the mattress, pushing my cock deeper inside her.

"Yes!" she gasps as her cunt contracts around me. Watching her lose control like that does something to me. It releases the barrier holding me back. I follow her almost simultaneously, grunting my release as I fill the condom. I see stars for a moment, my vision darkening for a split second.

Fuck.

My rhythm stutters as I struggle to keep pace while my orgasm rolls through me. I manage one final thrust before collapsing on top of her, my chest heaving. Sweat glistens on my skin—and on hers too. I can feel her heart racing beneath me.

I don't want to crush her, so I find my strength, and on wobbly arms, I push off her, rolling over onto the mattress next to her. On my back, I stare up at the ceiling, my heart racing. Tingles run down my arms and my legs feel weak.

"That was…" she breaks off.

Incredible. It was incredible. "Best sex I've ever fucking had," I tell her.

She smiles. "Really?"

"Really, babe. I thought I was going to pass the fuck out."

She laughs. "You did not."

I don't confirm the truth of my statement. I just lean over and press a kiss to her cheek. "So fucking glad I saw you tonight."

"Me too. I was having a shitty time before… this."

I need to take care of the condom, but I pull her against me instead. I want to feel her against me. I want her close.

She snuggles against my side, her hand moving over my waist. I could lie wrapped in her for days.

"Do you want me to leave?" she asks, surprising the fuck out of me. I am not giving those vibes at all.

"What I want, babe, is to give my cock a break before we go in for round fucking two."

Her lips curl up at the corners. "Vigorous, aren't you?"

I place a finger under her chin. "For your pussy, yeah, I am."

Elyse leans forward and presses her mouth to mine. I squeeze her tit as I kiss her back. She pushes her pussy against my flaccid cock, rolling her hips, as if desperately seeking friction.

Forget waiting, I can eat her cunt while my cock recovers.

"What are you doing?" she asks as I move down the bed.

"Having fun." I give her a heated glance before I dive back between her folds.

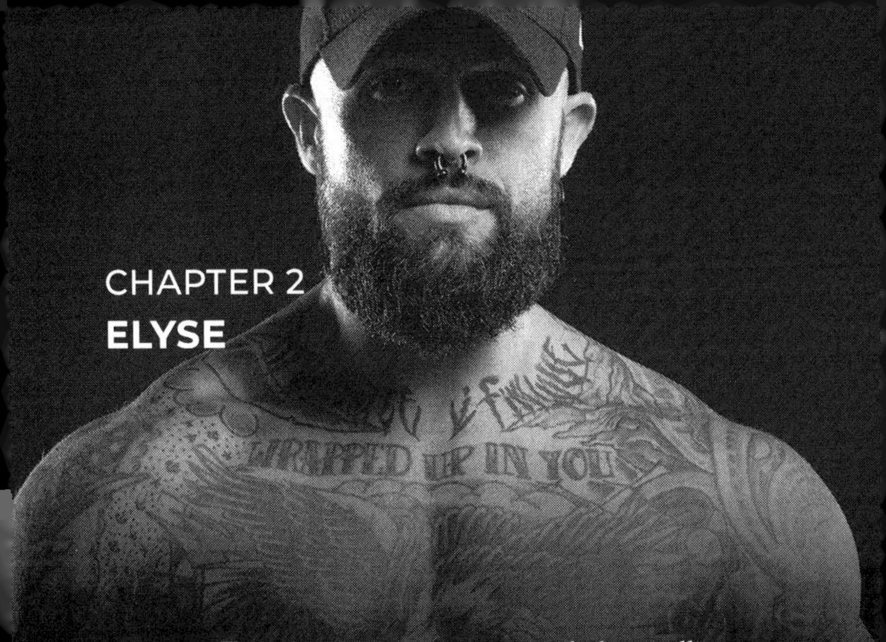

CHAPTER 2
ELYSE

Matt's breathing is even and slow, telling me he's out of it. I peer over at the man who rocked my freaking world last night, a pang of regret inching through my chest. He was good to me. Too good really. I don't deserve what he gave me. I shouldn't have taken it, but as soon as he asked me to come upstairs, I knew where the night was heading. Then was the time to back off.

But I wanted him.

It was selfish.

It was also the first selfish thing I've done in months.

Fucking a stranger isn't something I've done before, but I can't say I didn't like it. Matt was… amazing.

Guilt slices through me as I stare up at the ceiling, the sheets pulled up over my bare breasts. Am I really going to do this?

Blackjack…

He told me that was his club name.

That should have been enough to make me run. The man is in an MC—not just any MC either. The Untamed Sons. I know of them—everyone in Manchester does. They dominated the media for months. Gang warfare. The news reporters called it civil war on the streets.

If I do this, there's no turning back. I doubt he's going to let me walk away without consequences.

I don't have a choice. I don't have time to find another mark, not before he comes calling.

No. This has to happen now.

I take a deep breath, steeling myself for what I must do.

I can do this.

I have to do this.

Carefully, I slip out of the bed, my eyes gravitating towards Matt as the mattress shifts beneath my changing weight. His eyes are still closed, his breathing even.

He looks even bigger in the early morning light. His shoulders are broad, like a tank, and his tattoos look amazing. I wish I had time to study them all, but I need to get gone before he wakes up.

Finding my dress pooled on the floor, I snatch it up and quickly wriggle back into it, cursing at how little stretch the material has. That had been the aim of it last night, but I'm having to contort like a pretzel to get back into it.

When my dress is finally in place, I go to his jeans and pick them up, wincing when the belt clinks. A glance at the bed tells me he's still asleep.

I rummage through his pocket and find his stack of

winning chips. There's at least ten grand here. It isn't enough to pay the debt owed, but it'll keep the dogs at bay until I can come up with a new plan.

I hope.

I take the chips and grab my shoes, as well as my clutch bag. Then I sneak out of the room. I have to be fast. I need to collect the winnings and get out of here before he realises I've gone with his money.

I reach the door, my hand on the knob.

"You fucking cunt."

Matt's voice makes me freeze, my stomach flipping inside out. Shit, shit, shit.

I spin around, scared to have my back to him in case he launches at me. He's standing at the end of the bed, naked. He doesn't seem to care about that as he pins me with his eyes.

"So, you fucked me just to rob me?" The flat tone of his voice scares me more than if he shouted. My breath rips out of me as my mind races. He's going to kill me.

He's a biker.

He knows how to hide a body, I'm sure.

"Please don't hurt me," I whisper, fear clogging my words in my throat.

Matt laughs, but there's no humour behind it. "You steal from me, then ask me not to fucking hurt you. Do I look fucking lenient to you?"

He crosses the room in two long strides. I back up, my spine hitting the door behind me as his fingers wrap around my throat. His grip is strong, unrepentant, and I have no choice but to meet his eyes as he steps into my space. Fire burns in his irises as he bears down on me.

I'm too frightened to reply, too concerned I might say something that makes this situation worse—not that it can get much worse.

"You done this before?" he snarls.

"No."

"I don't believe a fucking word that comes out of your lying whore mouth."

"I'm not lying." I'm not. This is my first time ever doing anything like this, and desperation is the only reason I'm here.

"You think I'd be an easy mark?"

"I was desperate." It isn't a lie.

He tightens his grip on my neck, and I have to lean back slightly to relieve the pressure he's exerting.

"I could fucking end your life for this."

I hold my hand out, offering him the chips clutched between my fingers. It's death to give him them. If I turn up without any money, they will kill me, but if I don't give Matt this offering now, I'm going to die in this hotel room.

"Ain't about the fucking money, bitch."

He slams his fist into the wood next to my head, even as his other hand remains locked around my throat. I flinch, my breath rasping out of me.

"Why did you need the money?"

"Does it matter?"

"Yeah, Elyse, it fucking matters."

"I just need it."

Finally, he releases his hold on my throat and steps back, his body vibrating with rage. "Fucking bitches. You're all the same. Out for what you can get."

"It's not like that."

"Then what's it like?"

I lick my lips, my mouth dry. "I need it to protect someone I love very much."

"Is that supposed to pull at my fucking heart strings?" he demands, scooping his boxer briefs off the floor and pulling them on.

"No. But it's the truth. If I don't have the money, I don't know what will happen."

Matt casts a sidelong glance at me. "You could have asked for it."

This makes me scoff. "Right, and you'd have just handed it over. No questions asked. To a complete stranger."

The look on his face tells me he wouldn't have done that at all.

"I'm sorry, Matt. I really never intended to hurt you."

"Take the money and fuck off." He gives me his back, his dismissal stinging more than I care to admit.

"Matt—"

He rounds on me, his eyes spitting fire. "I see you again, I'll fucking put a bullet in you."

I believe he will. I don't move instantly, pain running through my body. "For what it's worth, I'm sorry."

"Go, before I change my fucking mind."

I reach for the handle and slip out of the room. As soon as it shuts behind me, I sag against the door, allowing myself a moment to relish the fact I'm still breathing. Fuck. I can't do this again. I can't. The stress…

I rush up the corridor towards the stairs. I'm too scared to wait for the lift in case he changes his mind. I rush down them as fast as I can bare foot. When I reach the bottom step, I use the rail to hold me up while I slip my heels on.

Then I walk into the casino as if I own the world. My head is held high, my back straight, my confidence oozing out of me.

I make straight for the booth where the chips are exchanged for money, and I place Matt's winning chips on the counter.

The man behind the desk peers at them before raising his eyes to mine. I see the doubt, the suspicion as I push them closer. "I need to cash these in."

He doesn't move for a moment, then he slides off his stool and disappears into the back.

It feels like it takes three hundred years for him to return, and when he does, he has a neat stack of notes banded together with a label declaring it is the ten grand I estimated.

I swallow hard but force a smile as he hands the money over. I stare at the pile of fifty-pound notes for a moment, before I shove it into my bag. It takes a little manoeuvring to get it to fit, but I just about manage.

I give the man behind the desk a forced smile before I head for the doors. The entire time I expect someone to stop me, for Matt to appear and say I'm stealing his money. Terror climbs up my spine with each step I take towards freedom, and I don't breathe until I push through the revolving door and step out onto the pavement.

I breathe the fresh air, ignoring the chill, and grab the nearest cab pulled up outside the building. I give the driver my address, and I don't relax until the casino is in the rear-view mirror. I clutch my bag to me, the money that could save my brother's life nestled inside.

Howard wants twenty grand by the end of the week. Ten will have to suffice because there is no way in hell I'm doing that again. I used up my one free pass. I don't want to end up in a ditch.

Carefully, I extradite some money from the bottom of my bag—not from the winning bundle—ready to pay my taxi fare. When the cab stops outside my flat, I hand over the money and climb out. I don't give a shit that it's barely six a.m. and I am wearing last night's clothes. I don't even care I'm dressed ready for a night out.

My only focus is getting safely inside with the money burning a hole in my bag.

I fumble to get the key in the lock, but after a second, it gives and the door opens. As soon as I step inside the hallway, I slam the door shut behind me.

Then I breathe.

Fuck. I suck back as much air as I can, my heart racing. My palms are sweaty—the back of my neck too.

"Elyse?"

I spin at the voice and see my brother standing in the doorway. His dark hair is messy, and his shirt is baggy on him. He's twelve, but already taller than I am. My hand presses against my heart.

"Shit, you scared me."

"Where've you been?" he demands.

I step into the living room of our small flat. It's tiny, barely big enough for the both of us, but it's all I can afford on my wages. It's more than I can afford really. I sleep on the sofa while Aaron has the small bedroom.

"You didn't come home last night. I was worried."

Fuck. I didn't want him to worry. "I thought you'd be in bed. I'm sorry. I should have messaged."

"So where were you?"

I toss the money onto the coffee table. "Getting that."

Aaron's eyes move to the cash before raising to meet my gaze. "How?"

"Does it matter? It'll hold Howard at bay—for a little while." I hate that he knows about Howard. I hate that he's involved in this shit storm at all, but Howard didn't care about protecting a vulnerable preteen from this nightmare. Aaron has witnessed more than I've been able to protect him from.

He sinks onto the armchair, clasping his hands between his parted legs. He stares at the money, as if he's scared to touch it. "How much is it?"

"Ten grand."

His eyes flare. "Where did you get it?"

I don't answer. Instead, I go to the sofa—my bed—and flop onto it. As I toe my heels off, Aaron sits forward and picks up the money. He flicks through the notes.

"Fuck, Elyse. What did you do?"

"Language," I chastise. "Don't you worry about what I did. It's taken care of and that's all that matters." I run my fingers through my hair, pushing it off my face. I want a shower. I want to sleep too. I didn't get any last night between being fucked all night by Matt and waiting for him to fall asleep. I'll never tell Aaron what I had to do to get that money. I'll never tell him I slept with a total stranger for ten grand. It isn't even enough to cover what Howard asked for, but I can't go back to the casino. I believe Matt when he said he'd kill me if he sees me again.

Fucking Dad.

If I could get my hands on him, I'd beat the shit out of him for putting us both in this situation.

Aaron forces out a breath, his eyes heavy with emotion. "This isn't your problem. Isn't right he's coming after you." It isn't, but what am I supposed to do? Howard's made it my problem. "If we can just find Dad—"

I laugh. "Kid, Dad's long gone." He is. We haven't seen him in months. I looked for him at first—of course, I did—but he was long gone. No one knows where he went, and if they do, they aren't telling me.

"You shouldn't have to do this. It's not fair."

It isn't, but life isn't fair either. For whatever reason, Howard decided I was responsible for all our father's outstanding gambling debts. Dad always had a weakness for the horses, but I never knew how bad that issue was until he disappeared one night, and Howard turned up, demanding two hundred and fifty thousand pounds.

Howard threatened my brother's life as well as my own if I didn't pay it. At first, he was content with a small amount from my wages each month, but out of the blue last week, he demanded more. He wanted twenty grand back. Even if I saved all year, I couldn't pay him that back.

It was that desperation that put me in the casino last night, willing to open my legs to steal what I needed. It was a whole new low for me, but what was I supposed to do? We could disappear too, but we don't have the money to truly live under the radar—not when Howard has means to find us.

My phone starts to ring, and we both freeze. I open my bag and pull my phone out.

"It's him?" he asks quietly.

I nod and swipe the phone to answer it. "Bedroom, now."

Aaron ignores me, and I have no choice but to answer the phone with him still in the room or risk missing the call. Howard would kill me for that slight alone.

"You have the money?" Howard's slimy voice sounds down the line. I push up from the sofa and move into the kitchenette, trying to gain some distance between me and Aaron. He doesn't need to hear this or worry about it.

I'm twenty-two and the adult here.

Not him.

He's a kid and he deserves to act like one.

I've failed him so badly by even letting him know this problem exists, though that was Howard's doing too.

"I have some of it," I admit, holding my breath as silence fills the line.

"If I'd wanted some of it, I would have fucking asked for some of it."

I close my eyes and try to calm my racing heart. "You

know I don't have that kind of money, Howard. I got what I could."

"How much?"

"Ten grand."

"You're ten short."

"I'm doing my best."

"It isn't enough."

"Please..." my breath clogs in my throat.

"I'll be at your flat within the hour. Be there."

The line goes dead, and fear clutches my chest. I pull my phone from my ear and close my eyes as I try to find my equilibrium.

"Elyse?"

I force a smile. "You're going to Jordan's."

He scowls. "Why?"

"Because I said so and it's good for you to be with your friends."

"I'm not leaving you to deal with that prick."

"What did I say about your language? Go. Now."

Muttering under his breath, he pushes up and storms off to his bedroom. I head to the bathroom. The tub is enamel, not plastic, old and rusted in places. Around the plug hole is orange and grimy. I've tried to clean it with every substance I can get my hands on, but the entire bathroom suite needs replacing.

I twist the knobs for the shower. The pipes clang, as they always do before the water lets down. I undress and step under the spray, ignoring the fact the water is barely tepid.

It feels criminal to wash a man like Matt off me, but I

lather up the soap and rub it over my body, removing every last trace of him. I wash my pussy, feeling sore and achy there. He was an unforgettable presence; one I'll never repeat.

I push Matt out of my head and focus instead on Howard. He'll be here soon and I need to be dressed before he is.

I wash my hair and rinse the soap out before I switch the water off and climb out of the tub. I wrap the towel around my body and leave the bathroom. In the living room, I pause and listen. I can't hear any sounds coming from Aaron's room, so I assume he did as I asked and went to Jordan's. He lives on the first floor of the building with his grandmother. They both go to the same school and have been friends since I took my brother in.

The chest of drawers behind the sofa has my clothes in, so I grab a clean pair of jeans and a hoodie. I dry myself before I get dressed. I put my dress from last night in the laundry. It's a throwback to a time before preteens and deadbeat parents ruled my life.

I'm just brushing my damp hair when there's a knock on the front door. My hands start to shake, but I clamp them together as I cross the living room and step into the small hallway. I pause at the door, wondering why I'm doing this.

Because what choice is there?

If I go to the police, it will cause more trouble than I'm already in. Howard isn't a man to screw with.

I let out a breath before I slide the lock back and open the door.

Before I can say a word, Howard pushes into the flat. He's a big guy, though at least four inches shorter than Matt. He's not as broad either, but he can hurt me if he chooses to. I am no match for him, and he knows it. It's why he comes alone. It's a show of power. He doesn't need anyone to protect him—not from me. His dark hair is kept short, and he has an ugly scar across his throat. I've never asked about it, but I'd guess he didn't get it from being a good person.

He shoves the door shut behind him, encroaching into my space as he backs me down the hallway and into the living room.

"The money, Elyse."

Right. The money. I pick up the stack off the table and hand it to him. His brow cocks at the band holding the notes together. "Where'd you get this?"

"Does it matter?"

He flips through the notes and breaks the band as he steps over to the chest of drawers. Slowly, he counts the pile. I watch, my stomach churning.

After a few minutes, he gathers the piles he's counted out together and pockets them in his jacket pocket.

When he turns back to me, my fear jumps up a notch. The look on his face is enough to twist the screws of fear.

"Thanks for the payment, but it's a little short."

"I told you it was. That's all I could get—"

He holds a hand up, and I fall silent. "Payment must be met, sweetheart. I'm not running a charity here."

"I don't have anything else to give you."

His eyes crawl up and down my body, lingering on my

breasts even though they are hidden under the baggy shape of the hoodie I pulled on after my shower. I can't stop from covering myself with my arms.

He steps up to me. "If you don't have the money, then we have a problem."

"I can get you more. It'll take time." My voice sounds desperate, and I hate that it does, but I am.

"I don't like to wait, Elyse." He's so close to me now that I have to tip my head back to meet his eyes. I want to move back, but my feet are rooted to the carpet. His fingers reach out and cup my right breast through my hoodie. I suck in a breath, more from shock than anything. Sleeping with a stranger because I chose to is one thing. Matt was a means to an end, but I wanted what he gave me.

This is different.

Howard is touching me without permission.

I pull away, but he grabs my arm, stopping me. "Debts must be paid."

"It's not even my debt. Why the hell am I on the hook for it? Find my prick of a father and get your money back from—" I don't finish my rant. Howard slams his fist into my stomach. I double over, gasping for air as my whole body seems to stop breathing.

Fuck.

I've never been hit before, and it hurts. A lot.

He fists his fingers into my still damp hair, tugging my head back. Pain sears through my scalp, making my eyes water. "I missed the part where you get a fucking say. You owe me. You're ten grand short. Now I can take that shit out on your little brother, or you can pay it back in another way."

Not Aaron. Fuck, not my brother. "He's just a kid," I rasp.

"You're not leaving me a lot of fucking choices here, Elyse."

I lick my lips, trying to move into him to loosen some of the pressure on the roots of my hair. "What do you want?"

"I want you to suck my cock."

I blink. Did I… did I hear him correctly?

"No."

"Then I'll find your brother and I'll fucking bury him in the deepest, darkest fucking hole I can find."

My heart is racing, and the back of my neck feels too warm as I shake my head. This can't be real. I won't let him touch my brother, but…

Sucking his cock?

Disgust floods me. He doesn't give me the chance to argue. He shoves me down to my knees, releasing his hold on my hair so he can undo his trousers.

Everything feels like it's slowed, and the room has narrowed to a pinpoint—his crotch. He unzips and pulls his thick cock out. It's flaccid as he grabs my hair again and forces my mouth around it.

"Bite it and I'll kill your brother in front of you before I slit your fucking throat."

His threat is enough to make me hollow my cheeks so I can take him. He slides deep into my throat, hitting my gag reflex. I choke, my mouth filling with saliva, but he holds my head firm, stopping me from pulling back as he fucks my mouth ruthlessly. Tears roll down my cheeks as I struggle to breathe around his cock, which is starting to harden in my mouth. I'm suffocating on his fucking dick and there's nothing I can do because he's holding me so tight.

I try to focus on the rhythm he's set, moving in time with his thrusts and keeping my teeth out of the way in case he really follows through on his threat.

I endure what feels like an eternity of him fucking my mouth like I'm a cheap whore. I feel like one too. On my knees, in my living room slash bedroom, a cock in my mouth.

His grunts of pleasure make my stomach twist and nausea climb up my throat.

Don't puke...

Don't puke...

He thrusts his hips one last time and spills cum into my mouth. I choke again, this time from his spunk coating my tongue and throat. He tastes salty, disgusting, and my skin crawls as I'm forced to swallow it down or choke further.

Howard thrusts a couple more times before pulling out of me, and I take my first unhindered breath in minutes.

I sink back onto the floor, my legs folded beneath me uncomfortably. It doesn't matter. I don't feel it or anything but the pounding of my heart.

Howard tucks himself into his trousers and zips back up.

"I'll be back in a month for another twenty grand."

Is he serious? "I can't… Howard, you know I don't have access to that kind of money—"

"Then I guess you'll be on your knees again, won't you?"

He leaves the flat, closing the front door behind him. Tears roll down my cheeks, my skin crawling as shock washes over me. What the fuck…

I wipe at my mouth, still tasting him.

Then I stagger to my feet and rush to the bathroom, where I throw my guts up.

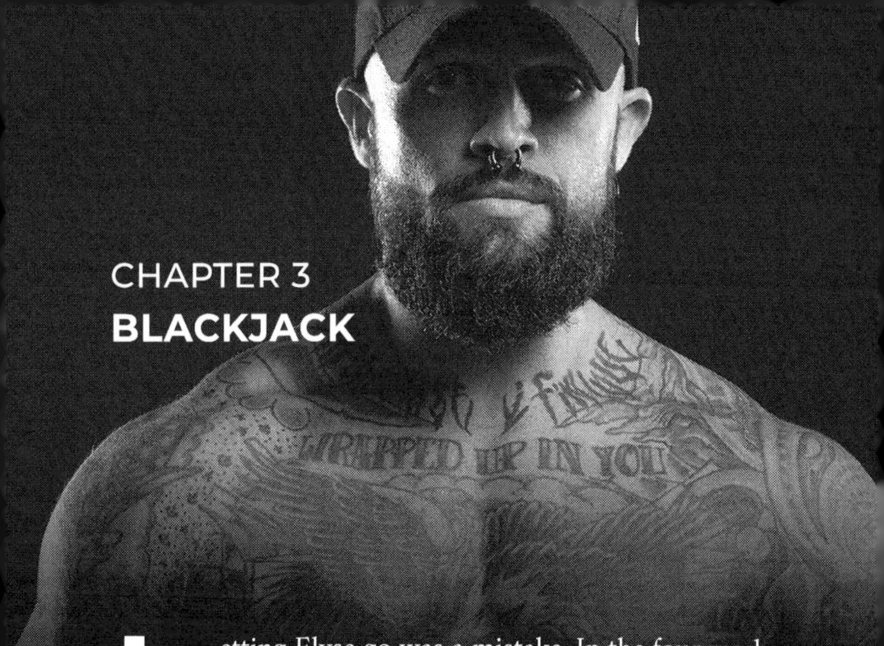

CHAPTER 3
BLACKJACK

Letting Elyse go was a mistake. In the four weeks since I allowed her to walk out of my hotel room with my money, she's all I've been able to think of. I don't care that she stole ten grand from me. The money isn't the fucking issue.

It's her.

I shouldn't give a fuck about my little thief, but why did she need it? She risked getting hurt. Had she chosen any other mark, she could have been. I let her walk away. I shouldn't have but I did. I still don't know why I did that.

The more I think about it, the more pissed I become. I shouldn't have let her walk out of that room without consequences.

It made me look weak.

It made the Sons look weak.

What could I have done though? I don't hurt women—even thieving cunts. Ain't in me to do that, but I could have done… something.

"You done with the motor yet?" Socket asks, dragging my thoughts back into the present.

I'm in the club's garage. The business sits at the top of the street, where the clubhouse is located, and is just one of the many legal fronts we use to wash the money we make through crime. It's Socket's baby, but I help out when I can. My duties as vice president keep me busy, but I like to get lost under a bonnet when I need a break.

"Another five minutes and I'll be finished," I say.

He wipes his greasy hands on a rag and studies me. "You okay, brother?"

"Shouldn't I be asking you that?"

His reunion with his daughter hasn't been as straight forward as I think he'd hoped. We'd pulled Pia out of a rival club's clubhouse after she was taken by their president, Wrecker, to pay a debt her ex-husband owed.

No one knew Socket had a kid. Not until his old flame Valentina turned up, begging for help.

We'd razed the Road Jesters' clubhouse to the ground, rescued Pia, and brought her back to the clubhouse while we searched for Wrecker. That fucker escaped in the commotion of us storming the building. Slippery fuck.

We found him eventually. Socket—and Howler—took his time dealing justice for his daughter. Then he sought to rebuild the bridges he'd destroyed by keeping his distance over the years.

Pia hasn't been exactly forgiving though. I don't blame that anger. I'd be furious if my family lied to me for years. Socket had his reasons for what he did—even if they were misguided. He was looking at a long time in prison.

Fifteen years. Pia would have been grown by then and he didn't want to change the world she knew. It's bullshit, but I'd never tell Socket that. The brother already gives himself a hard enough time about his actions without me adding to his guilt.

For months, he and Pia have been rebuilding their relationship a day at a time, but I don't think it's going as fast as he'd like.

Socket snorts. "Made my bed. Got to fucking lie in it now."

"Pia'll come around," I reassure him. "She already is."

"Yeah, she's giving me a chance, which I can't fucking believe. She doesn't owe me shit, but she's trying. Truthfully, Blackjack, I don't know if I can ever fix the hurt I caused her."

"Give it time," I say.

"I'll be the first to admit, I wasn't keen on her and Howler together, but he's good for her. She's grounded with him, and I know that fucker would defend her to his last breath. I feel better knowing that shit."

Pia and Howler had taken an almost instant like to each other, and that relationship had grown stronger over the months she's been with us. Howler claimed her pretty much as soon as he could. They've been staying at the clubhouse, but I know Howler has been looking for a house or a flat for them. If they stay close to the clubhouse, it'll be the latter.

"They're good for each other," I agree.

"Had my doubts, but he's more than shown his love for my girl."

"Howler's a good man," I say. He is. I've known him a long time—first, when we were with the Sons in London and then after, when he came to Manchester. I stood at his side while he carved out our territory and made the city bow to the Untamed Sons' name. "What's after this job?"

"A back tyre replacement, new brake discs and a battery change. I should be able to do the brakes after I'm finished with this welding job, if you take the other two."

I nod and go back under the bonnet. I need to push that fucking bitch out of my head and focus. I get lost for a while; my hands busy while my mind is empty.

Then she drifts back into my consciousness.

I want to know who she is.

I don't know why I care.

She's a nobody.

A fucking thieving cunt.

She used sex to lower my inhibitions enough to rob me.

She tried to sneak out of the hotel room while I was asleep. She picked the wrong guy to do that with. Years in the Forces taught me to sleep lightly, so I knew the moment she left the fucking bed. I thought she was heading to the bathroom. I didn't realise she was stealing from me until I watched her take my winning chips.

Despite all that, she's locked firmly in my thoughts.

Why did she need the money?

She robbed me knowing I'm in the Sons.

Desperate or stupid?

I finish up the jobs I need to do before cleaning up and

showering in the back room of the garage. I shrug on my tee and kutte before pulling on my jeans and boots. Then I make the short walk to the clubhouse. I need to check in with Howler before heading home.

I find the president of the Untamed Sons Manchester Chapter sitting in the common room with Terror, our sergeant-at-arms and enforcer.

I give both men a lift of my chin as I sit at the table with them. Terror talks for a few about a run he just got back from before he makes himself scarce.

"Ravage called," Howler says as soon as we're alone.

That piques my interest, but it's not unusual. As the Sons National chapter president and our mother chapter, Ravage calls a lot.

"He doing okay?"

"He's got a shipment coming in from Tennessee."

Guns. That's what our American brothers deliver to us. We send coke and heroin to them. The heroin comes from Afghanistan and is top quality shit—at least before we cut it to double the profits. Our Spanish friends get coke from East Africa and trade it with their European friends. Ravage handles most of the incoming trade and we distribute what he gives us. Then we wash the money through our legal trades. It's a good system, one that keeps us all wealthy as fuck. That's why I didn't give a fuck about the ten grand Elyse stole from me—if that's even her real name.

It's pocket money. I could have lost that at the table and not blinked.

"Where do you need me?"

"You and Trick are going to Leicester."

Slasher is president of our Leicester chapter and a good brother. Loyal as fuck to the Sons.

"Got it."

Howler's eyes slide to the opposite side of the room, where Pia is sitting with her mother. She seems to know she's being watched, because her eyes meet his, and the way she looks at him makes me feel fucking envious. There's so much there. So much love. So much affection. So much everything. She stares at him like he's her reason for breathing.

Lissa saunters over, placing a lager in front of me, bringing my attention back to the bar, and a Scotch in front of Howler.

"Thanks, babe," Howler says, finally tearing his attention away from his old lady.

"You boys need anything else?" she asks.

She's wearing a tiny mini skirt that just about hides her cunt. She's not wearing underwear, but that's not unusual for a club whore. They like to be ready to go when a brother wants them.

"No, darlin'," I tell her.

She sashays away, the globes of her arse cheeks peeking out beneath the material. Fuck, I need to release some of this fucking tension in my bones. I need to get Elyse out of my brain.

"We done here?" I ask, my attention wandering back to Lissa as she moves behind the bar.

Howler nods, following my eyeline. "Ain't nothing but trouble there," he warns.

"Ain't looking to wife her, nor am I looking for an opinion." I clamp a hand on his shoulder before heading over to the bar.

Lissa glances up as I approach. "You busy?"

She places the glasses she was cleaning on the counter and steps around the bar. Her hands roam over my chest and my kutte, lingering on the vice president patch on my chest. "You want to have a little fun, Blackjack?"

I take her hand and lead her out into the corridor, heading towards her room. As soon as the door is shut behind us, she presses me against the wall, her hand rubbing over my cock, through my jeans.

"Do you want me to suck you off?" she asks.

I undo my jeans and tug down my boxer briefs. She takes my cock in her hand, but as soon as she touches me, it feels fucking wrong. Lissa gets to her knees, peering up at me through her lashes like a fucking porn star. Instead of her dark hair, I imagine red, but it doesn't work.

I grab her hand, stopping her from guiding me into her mouth.

"Fuck," I mutter. "Changed my mind."

I pull free from her grasp and zip my jeans up before stepping around her. She doesn't say a word in protest—she knows better—as I leave her on her knees.

I head outside, and as soon as the fresh air hits me, I feel pissed. Why the fuck is my little thief still on my mind?

I scrub a hand over my face. Fucking hell. I need to get a grip. I need to push her out of my head completely and let her go. So the sex was amazing. So there was a connection. None of it was real. She used me. She lured me up to that room to steal from me. If she'd been a man, I would have gutted her. She would never have left the casino alive.

As a rule, we don't hurt women. It's a club rule and one I'm fine with following—no innocents, no women. We don't hurt people not in the life. People who haven't chosen to cross the lines we do. I know I could die at any time. Tomorrow isn't promised. It hadn't been promised during the four years I served either. I was used to looking death in the face. I was used to death looking back with a fucking smile too.

Despite stealing from me, I got the impression Elyse is innocent. She didn't strike me as a career criminal, going to casinos to lift money from winners.

"Blackjack."

I peer up as Trick steps out, a cigarette hanging from his mouth. The brother is one of the few in the club to have an old lady. He and Mara were childhood sweethearts, married young, completely besotted with each other. I envy that.

"Hey."

I watch as he cups his cigarette to light it against the breeze.

"You got the Leicester run?"

"Yeah. Was supposed to be doing Cardiff, but it's Mara's birthday this weekend. I'm taking her on a city break."

Mara is Trick's old lady and a doctor. She's also the

sweetest fucking person I've ever met. I doubt she robs bikers in casinos.

Fuck.

"Sounds good, brother."

Maybe I need to take a trip of my own. Spend some time in London or Birmingham. Get lost for a while and put Elyse out of my head.

"Riding out," I mutter and make my way to my bike, which is parked out the front of the clubhouse.

I free my helmet from the lock and climb on. As I pull my keys from my pocket, I focus on the bike beneath me. The open road will sort my fucked-up head out.

I start the engine, and the rumbling soothes me in a way nothing else can.

I back the bike out of the space and align it with the road, ready to ride. I give Trick, who is still leaning against the front wall of the clubhouse, a lift of my chin, then I ride.

I don't have a destination in mind, but it doesn't matter. I ride until my mind is free and empty. I ride until I can no long picture Elyse's face.

I don't head back to my flat until the sun has set and nightfall is creeping in. As soon as I get inside, I grab a bottle of liquor from the cupboard, and then I drink until I pass out.

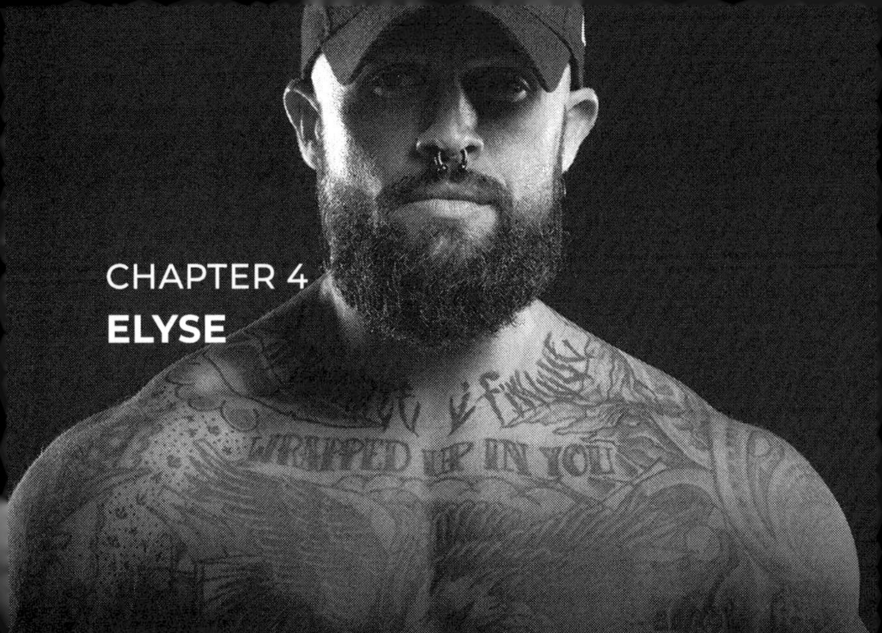

CHAPTER 4
ELYSE

Nausea climbs up my throat as Howard forces me to my knees again. I'm relieved Aaron isn't here to witness the lows I've sunk to, but I can't keep doing this. This is the third time he's expected me to drop to my knees and suck him off because I couldn't pay.

I'll never be able to pay.

Even if I sold every single thing I own, it wouldn't come close to what he's asking for.

I'm scared to go back to the casino in case Matt is there.

"Stop," I say as he pulls his cock out.

"You have the money?"

"No, but—"

He doesn't let me finish. He shoves his cock between my lips, his hand fisting into my hair to hold me in place. I choke instantly, trying to push back as he forces himself deep into my throat. Tears start to run down my face. I swallow down the urge to vomit. If I puke on his cock, Howard will kill me.

It feels like it lasts an eternity. Every thrust of his hips adds to the ugly, swirling feeling in my gut. I've become a whore. His whore. I don't know how much more of this I can take, but I don't know what the alternative is. If I don't pay or let him abuse me like this, what will he do to me, to my brother?

He doesn't take long to orgasm. His cum fills my mouth and I'm forced to swallow it. My skin crawls, and it feels like dirt covers every inch of me. The violation I have experienced makes me sick to my stomach.

I wipe my mouth, wanting to brush my teeth and rinse it out with bleach, but I'm too scared to move. Every bone in my body feels locked in position as I peer up at him, unsure what he's going to do next.

He grabs my arm, his touch rough. His fingers press hard enough against my skin to bruise. I try to pull away, but his ironclad grip keeps me in place. "I'll be back in a month. Next time, I want fifty grand, and if you can't deliver, it's going to take more than a blow job."

He pulls me to my feet, and without asking or invitation, he cups me between my legs. Fear like I've never felt zips through me as he rubs me through my clothes. It doesn't bring pleasure. I'm terrified of what he's going to do next. Giving that old prick a blow job every month is bad enough, but letting him touch me, letting him fuck me, is never going to happen.

He presses a kiss to my cheek, and I turn away, disgusted. It's a mistake. He grabs my chin between his finger and thumb. My jaw aches as he presses hard. He means to hurt me, as I have hurt him.

"I own you, Elyse. If I want to fuck your pretty cunt, there's nothing you can do to stop me."

He kisses me again, and this time, I don't move. I'm too scared to. "I'll see you in four weeks' time."

I watch as he goes to the door and steps out of the flat, numbness spreading through my body. Then I rush to the bathroom and throw up.

I have no idea what I'm going to do, but I try to keep things as normal as possible for my brother. I don't want Aaron to know what is going on. He already complains about the fact I make him leave every time Howard comes over. I don't know how much longer he will do as I ask, but I can't have my brother here when I'm being abused by this monster.

I sink back against the bathtub and catch my breath. I can't keep doing this. I despise my father for leaving us to deal with this.

I can't see a way out of it. Howard owns me. The threat of hurting Aaron is enough to make me compliant.

Up… I need to get up.

Forcing my legs to move, I push up from the bathroom floor and lean against the basin. I wash my face and brush my teeth, scrubbing my tongue until it feels sore.

After that, I shower, trying to wash the dirt off my skin. It sticks like molasses. It will always stick to me.

I text Aaron, telling him to be home before nine pm, then I head to work.

As well as my admin job during the day, I'm working nights at Rush, a local bar. It's hard work. I'm on my feet for hours, serving and clearing glasses, but I need as much money as I can get.

It's a fruitless exercise because I can never raise what Howard asks for. Even if I worked six jobs, it would never cover the debt, but I have to do something. Giving Howard everything from my wages from my admin job meant I couldn't afford to pay rent or bills. I got the second job to pay for those.

I'm usually tired, but tonight, when I step through the staff entrance, I'm dragging my feet. I can barely propel myself forwards. It's going to be a long night.

I head into the staff room and shrug out of my jacket, stashing it and my bag in my locker. I pull at the tiny hot pants that make up my uniform, hating the way they expose the globes of my arse. I hate the fitted tank top too. It makes my breasts look huge and men fucking stare.

I hate being ogled.

I need this job. I need it to keep my brother fed and safe.

Tears threaten to fall. I'm so tired of being strong. I'm so tired of everything. I want to fall apart. Instead, I swipe at my eyes, careful not to mess up my makeup, then I take a breath, trying to dislodge the exhaustion nipping at my heels.

As I make my way out to the bar, the music vibrates through the floor beneath my feet. The room is lit by strobing disco lights, and despite the time, the floor is filled with customers.

I slip around the back of the bar and give Melody, one of the servers, a smile as I move to serve my first customer. I take the order and have to ask him to repeat it. My brain feels foggy, unsettled.

Melody meets me at the back counter, reaching for a bottle of tequila as I reach up to put a shot of Vodka into the glass I'm clutching.

"Be warned, Frank's on the warpath tonight."

Frank is our boss. He's a misogynistic pig, but I'm grateful he gave me a chance.

"What's up with him?"

"Rach didn't show up for shift."

Rach is well known for skipping out on her obligation. If it was anyone else, Frank would have fired her, but Rach brings in a ton of custom. It would be enough to put our boss in a mood.

As I serve more and more people, I start to feel light-headed, like I'm floating on the floor. I stumble, and the glass I'm holding slides out of my fingers. It hits the floor, obliterating into a thousand pieces.

Frank moves to the end of the bar and signals me over. He's maybe forty, attractive, but his mouth is constantly pulled into a scowl. "That glass is coming out of your fucking pay," he yells across the bar.

I try to reply, but the dizziness is swamping me. My heart feels like it's pounding in my chest. I try to speak but no words come out. Then, it's lights out.

I wake up on the floor behind the bar, Melody

kneeling over me. Relief floods her face as I blink, trying to focus.

"Wh-what happened?" I ask, trying to sit up. She stops me with her hands on my shoulders. I'm too weak to stop her from pushing me back down.

"Stay still. The paramedics are on the way."

"Paramedics? I don't need that."

I try to move again and my head rolls. Fuck. I'm so dizzy. My vision is blurry, and my heart is thudding, fluttering frantically.

"You need to be checked over."

Frank crowds in. "Get her up," he hisses.

Melody gives him a heated glare. "As soon as someone with a medical degree says she can."

Frank throws his hands in the air. "This is what I get for dealing with bitches."

I lie still, ignoring him and focusing on breathing. My heart is still racing, and I feel sick to my stomach. It feels like it takes forever for the paramedics to arrive, and by the time they do, I'm starting to feel worse.

The lead paramedic moves to me, kneeling beside me.

"What happened?"

"She passed out," Melody supplies.

The paramedic gives me a warm smile. "What's your name, sweetheart?"

"Um... Elyse Taylor."

He nods as he opens his medical kit and wraps a blood pressure cuff around my bicep. "That happened before?"

I shake my head.

"You have any medical conditions?"

"No."

"When was the last time you ate?" Recovering that detail is harder than it should be.

"This… afternoon? What day is it?"

"Friday. Are you pregnant?"

"No."

"Other than fainting, do you have any other symptoms?"

"I'm dizzy. A little nauseous. Everything is blurry. My heart… It's really pumping." I press my hand to my chest, as if it can slow it down.

"Like a palpitation?"

"Yeah. It feels like it's going to beat out of my chest."

The machine beeps, and he turns to look at the read out. He keeps his expression soft, but I can see the concern in his eyes. "Your blood pressure is low, Elyse. I'm not happy with how low. I want one of our doctors to check you over at the hospital."

The hospital? I can't go to the fucking hospital. Frank will sack me.

"Hang on, is that fucking necessary?" he demands. "I'm already a member of staff down."

The paramedic turns to glare at him. "She needs to go to the hospital."

Frank glares back. "This is my business—"

"She's going, and if you get in my way, we're going to have a problem," he grinds out.

"You go and you're fired," he says to me.

My heart sinks. "I don't need to see a doctor," I tell the

paramedic. I need this job more than I need to be checked over.

"Elyse, your blood pressure is dangerously low. Even if you stay, you're going to have a repeat of this. You can't sustain your body with your numbers this low. You're just going to keep passing out."

Fuck.

"It might be nothing, but it could be something to worry about," he says in a soft voice. "You can get another job. You can't get another life."

If I die, Aaron will end up in the care system.

It's that thought that makes me nod. "Okay."

Ignoring Frank's grumbling, the paramedics get me onto a trolley and wheel me out to the ambulance.

Once I'm loaded in the back, the paramedic who stood up to Frank gets in the back with me, his partner driving.

"What's wrong with me?" I ask him as he puts an oxygen mask over my face. As I breathe it in, I start to feel less dizzy.

"Well, that's what we're going to find out," he says, giving me a reassuring smile.

By the time we reach the hospital, I'm starting to feel a little better. I'm wheeled into a cubicle, and medical personnel swarm me. The paramedic reels off the things wrong with me and then questions are fired at me as they hook me up to an ECG machine. Bloods are taken from the crook of my arm too. I lose track of the paramedic, not seeing him anywhere in the room.

The doctor is a beautiful woman with the warmest

smile I've ever seen. "We're going to fix you up," she assures me.

A nurse hands her a printout, which she takes a moment to look at. "Well, the good news is whatever is causing your low blood pressure doesn't look like a heart issue. The question is: what is? We're going to run some tests, see if we can get to the bottom of it. For now, we're going to get some fluids into you and try to raise your pressure. Is there anyone we can call for you?"

Aaron knows I'm working and isn't expecting me home until late. He will be asleep by then. I shake my head. "There's no one."

"Have you had this happen before?"

"No, but I'm… tired. I've been tired for a few weeks now. I thought I was just working too hard."

"What do you do for a living?"

"I work in an office and a bar."

She smiles. "Try to relax. We'll be back soon."

The doctor disappears, leaving me with a nurse, who gets me comfortable and changed into a hospital gown. I don't want to sleep, but I'm so tired I find myself drifting off.

"Elyse." The voice makes my eyes open. I come face to face with the doctor who treated me when I first came in. "I have some of your results back."

She pulls up a stool so she can sit at the edge of the bed. The nurse who was with me earlier is gone, the curtains pulled around the bed, giving the illusion of privacy, even though I can hear the bustle of the emergency room behind it.

I shift in the bed, sitting up more. My head rolls a little, my vision blurring.

"Still dizzy?"

"A little. It's better than it was. Am I sick?" The thought makes my stomach churn. If I'm sick, who will take care of my brother?

"No, you're not sick." Her assurance makes me breathe a sigh of relief.

"So why did I pass out?"

"Your blood pressure dropped low, which gave you the symptoms you experienced."

"So, I'm sick?"

"You're pregnant."

For a moment, her words echo through my brain. Pregnant. I'm pregnant.

Is she crazy?

I shake my head.

"No, I can't be."

Sympathy crosses her face. "This wasn't planned?"

"Not even a little. I'm not… I'm not even seeing someone." That makes me sound like a slut. My cheeks pink. "I mean… I don't sleep around. Though I did have a—"

A one-night stand.

With a biker.

A dangerous biker who threatened to end my life if he saw me again.

"You do have options. I can go through them with you if you'd like."

"Abortion?" An ugly feeling spreads through me at the thought.

"Or adoption."

My hand strays to my flat belly. Beneath my hand, a child is growing.

My child.

Mine and Matt's child.

My brain is a mess as I let that thought sink in. "How… how many weeks? Can you tell?"

She peers down at her notes. "From the hCG levels I'd estimate between eight to nine weeks. We need to do an ultrasound to be certain. When was your last period?"

I try to think back. "I had one…" I frown. "I don't remember. Things have been stressful. I didn't keep track."

"It's okay. Let's do an ultrasound and see how the baby looks."

I nod, feeling numbness spread through me. I can't look after me and Aaron, let alone a newborn. How am I going to work? How am I going to do anything?

She disappears behind the curtain and returns a moment later with a machine on wheels. "Can you put your legs in the stirrups for me?"

I do as she asks, feeling exposed with my legs spread like this. My heart feels like it's going to explode out of my chest for real this time.

Pregnant.

I'm pregnant.

What the fuck am I going to do?

I can't keep a baby.

I can't go to Matt for help either—not after his threats.

If I keep this baby, I will be alone.

If?

What am I thinking? I can't keep it. I'm barely treading water as it is.

"Your baby is going to be too small to be seen on a routine ultrasound, so I'll take a look transvaginally. It's not as scary as it sounds. It's a little wand that I insert inside you, and we can have a look around."

She pulls the stool to the end of the bed and lifts the blankets up. I peer at the ceiling, feeling like I'm in a dream. How am I sitting in a hospital cubicle, my legs akimbo, a doctor inserting a device into my pussy?

I wince as it enters but try not to tense up.

"Okay, let's have a look." The doctor's voice is calm, reassuring, but I feel anything but. My heart is hammering once again beneath my ribs.

I peer at the grainy screen, unsure what the hell I'm looking for. It looks like television static. There's nothing baby-shaped.

"I don't see anything," I say.

"At this stage, we won't see much. Baby is still in early phases of development. We might see something that looks vaguely like the right shapes."

She moves the wand inside me, but my focus is on the screen. "Ah, there's Baby." She points to two little oval shapes on the screen.

I blink. "That's my baby?" The emotions that flood me are indescribable. I've never felt anything like it. It's like pure joy rolls through me, a hit of endorphins that steals my breath. All the fear I felt, dissipates as I stare at those little blobs on the screen.

"That's your baby," the doctor confirms.

I feel like I'm having an out of body experience. Awe fills me. For weeks my baby has been growing inside me and I had no idea. It does explain how I've been feeling though. The exhaustion. The general malaise.

I'm pregnant.

I swipe at the tears on my face, feeling suddenly overwhelmed by everything. "Is he or she okay?"

"Everything looks as it should, but I want you to see your own doctor at twelve weeks, just to get a proper look at Baby then."

"Shouldn't I hear the heartbeat?" I've watched enough medical TV shows over the years to know that's a big part of ultrasounds.

"It can take a few more weeks before that happens, but everything looks perfect. I'd say you are more towards the eight-week mark than nine."

Which fits with the time I was with Matt—unsurprisingly. He's the only person I've slept with in a while.

She pulls the wand out of me. "Are you sure there isn't someone I can call for you?"

I shake my head.

"The baby's father?"

"That's complicated."

"It's probably less complicated than you think. People surprise us. You can put your legs down now."

She has no idea who I bedded.

"When can I go home?" I ask, lowering my legs.

"Once your blood pressure stabilises. We should be able to treat this at home though. Plenty of fluids, rest, good diet and it should sort itself out. If not, we can medicate, but let's see how we get on first."

I nod, and as soon as she steps around the curtain, I flop back against the pillow.

What the fuck am I going to do?

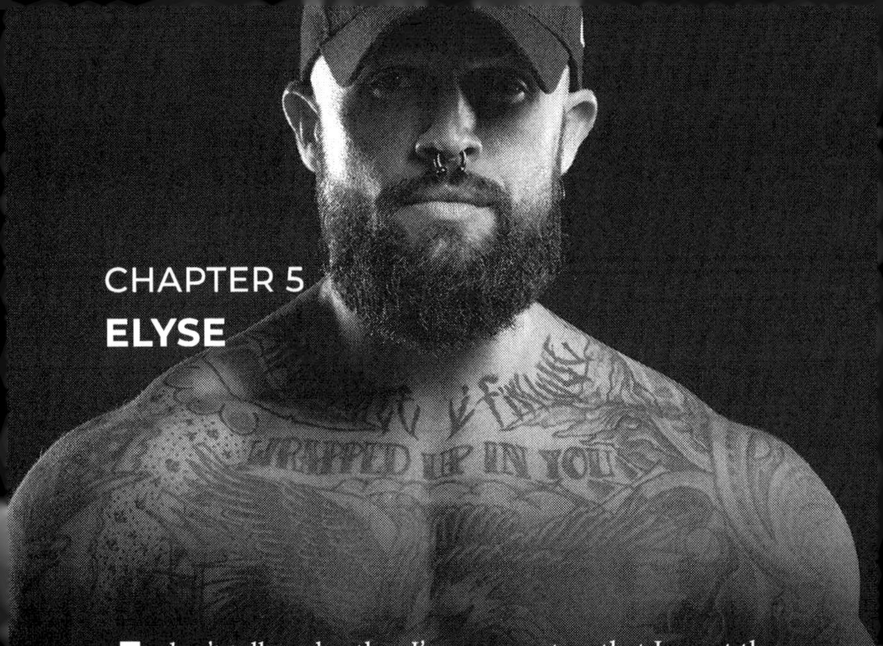

CHAPTER 5
ELYSE

I don't tell my brother I'm pregnant or that I spent the night in the hospital. The doc discharges me after a few hours, giving me a ton of leaflets on pregnancy and how to keep my blood pressure stable. There are things I need—medications I'm supposed to take to keep my baby healthy.

I haven't been able to stop thinking about what I'm going to do from the moment I found out. I want to keep my baby. I know that much. The thought of aborting it doesn't feel right, but I also can't afford to bring a child into the world. I'm already taking care of a child. Aaron needs me too.

I also have Howard and his threats in my head.

He's going to rape me the next time he comes to collect his money.

He said as much.

Sucking his dick is one thing. Letting him inside me…

The thought makes me sick.

One of the nurses slips me some money to take a taxi home. I'm glad because I still feel weak and exhausted.

I'm supposed to be at my office job, but I messaged my boss that I was at the hospital, sick. Unlike Frank, she was worried and told me to take as long as I need off. I have the day to myself.

I need to work out my next step.

When I get back into the flat, it's silent. Aaron is gone—at school—though the remnants of his breakfast dishes are piled in the sink. I wash up as I let my thoughts wander.

Howard will be back in a few weeks' time.

If it was just me to think about, it wouldn't matter, but now I have a baby in my belly. I need to protect him or her.

Whatever it takes.

The only thing that matters to me is keeping my child and my brother safe.

There is only one person who can help with that.

Matt.

When you're facing a bully, the only way to defeat it is to bring a bigger bully along. Matt is in an MC. I know the reputation the Sons have. Everyone in this area does. I also know that means he is my best chance of survival.

He said he would kill me if he saw me again…

Would he really do it though?

I shake the suds off my hands and empty the sink. The weight of the world feels like it's resting on my shoulders. It's hard enough being responsible for me and Aaron. This baby complicates things.

Maybe a termination would be the smartest move.

Life wouldn't have to change.

Everything would stay the same. A baby will need things—things I can't afford.

I think back to that grainy ultrasound picture.

I can't.

I place a hand on my flat stomach. Already, I feel so much for this tiny little thing growing inside me.

That leaves one choice.

Ask the father of my baby to protect me and hope he won't do as he threatened—put a bullet in me.

I shower and get changed. There are a few little souvenirs from my hospital stay on my body. Tape over where my IV drip was in my arm, and I find a sticky pad from the ECG under my breast. I scrub myself clean, and by the time I get out, I'm exhausted.

I want to sleep, but I need to do this while I'm in this frame of mind. If I stop to think about it too long, I'll not be able to go through with it.

I take the bus from my flat to the clubhouse. I don't have the money to waste on a cab and there was barely any change from what the nurse at the hospital gave me.

The Untamed Sons Clubhouse is located in the Ancoats region of the city of Manchester, tucked down a cul-de-sac. As I approach, I can see the rows of chrome bikes lined up on the street against a backdrop of red brick. There's a guy leaning against the wall, smoking a cigarette. He looks terrifying. He's huge, with a shaved head and a mean look on his face.

I swallow hard, my stomach churning. Can I do this? Can I risk it all on the chance Matt might take pity on me?

What if he doesn't care that I'm pregnant?

What if he hurts me?

I peer up at the building, my heart starting to race, the back of my neck feeling too warm. It doesn't look threatening, but I know what lies on the other side of those doors.

Violence.

Criminality.

Murderers.

I know how dangerous these men are because I'd poked a snake and narrowly avoided being bitten by one of them.

I can't do this alone.

I don't want to do this alone.

My hand strays to my belly. It's still flat, but beneath my splayed fingers my baby is growing inside me. A baby I have to protect at all costs. I never thought about starting my own family. I have enough shit to deal with because of my brother, but from the moment I found out I was pregnant, my mindset shifted completely.

I will walk through the fires of Hell to keep my child safe.

I pull my bottom lip between my teeth and steel my spine.

The menacing-looking man watches me approach with disinterest. He's wearing a leather vest, the words 'Sergeant-at-Arms' on the breast. His jeans are baggy, a chain running along his thigh, and he has a tattoo on his neck of a skull.

"You lost, sweetheart?" he asks when I stop in front of him.

I swallow my fear. "I'm looking for Matt."

He cocks a brow. "Matt."

"Blackjack," I say, remembering he told me that's what his brothers call him.

"Know who Matt is. Just wondering what a pretty little thing like you needs with my vice president."

He's their vice president? I don't know anything about how an MC hierarchy works, but that sounds pretty high up.

"I just need to talk to him. Please."

He eyes me like I'm a rabid dog before pushing his heel off the wall. I wait while he stubs his cigarette out, cold sweat clinging to my skin. My mouth suddenly feels dry.

"Follow me," he orders.

He leads me inside the building. My body feels electrified as I trail after him. The main doors open out onto a corridor with doors off it. I can hear music playing faintly in the background and the sound of laughter. The air feels too thin, like I can't draw it in. I feel light-headed as this man leads me through a set of double doors and into a bar area. There are tables scattered around the space, a pool table at one end, and what I think might be air hockey. A few men are gathered around a large TV watching a football match.

My eyes go to the long counter running the length of one wall. There are stools in front of it and two men sitting together. I can see the Untamed Sons insignia on the back of their leather vests—Manchester written underneath the image of a skull with wings and a crown. It's intimidating. Macabre.

I recognise Matt immediately, even though he has his back to me. He's a hulking man, bigger than the man he's sitting next to. If I wasn't so terrified, I would be glad to see him, hopeful of a repeat performance of what happened in the casino.

"Blackjack," the man who brought me into the clubhouse says.

Matt turns at the sound of his name, as does the man he's sitting with. Like Matt, he's in his thirties, with dark hair that flops into his eyes and tattoos on every inch of skin I can see.

I keep my focus locked on Matt as his gaze moves past his club friend to me. As soon as he spots me, rage burns through him. He stands abruptly, knocking the stool he was sitting on over. The noise it makes brings everyone's attention to us, and I feel like I'm being suffocated by those stares.

"Told you that if I saw you again, I'd fucking put a bullet in you. It wasn't a joke."

The anger in his voice scares me. I'm in the lion's den, facing down a predator. I pull my bottom lip between my teeth. He looks like he wants to wrap his hands around my neck and squeeze it.

"I know," I say, mindful of the men starting to drift towards us. "I wouldn't be here, except I need your help."

Matt closes the space between us and grabs my arm. It

hurts. I hold back my whimper as he pulls me away from the gathering crowd.

"You got a fucking death wish?" he hisses.

I don't. I want to live. That's why I'm here. "I need your help."

He stares at me with such hate I want to cry. I know what I did was bad, but I'm not a bad person. I was desperate.

"No," he snarls the word.

This is not going the way I need it to, and I'm starting to panic he's going to send me away without helping me.

"Please, Matt." I can't stop the needy inflection in my voice. I'm terrified of what Howard will do to me the next time he comes to collect.

Matt's eyes blaze. "Ain't fucking falling for that routine again, bitch. I learnt my fucking lesson." He drags me towards the doors. No. I can't leave. Not without help. I fight him, tugging against his hold, but he's got size and strength on his side. I'm weak after my collapse last night. Even if I were at full health, I doubt I could fight him.

"Let fucking go of me!" I try to twist out of his hold, but he doesn't release me. If anything, his grip tightens. The pain in my arm is reaching unbearable levels. It feels like he's going to snap the bone. "If I could take that back, I would."

"You can't."

My eyes dart around the room. I'm not in friendly territory. No one here is going to help me if he decides to hurt me, but I can't leave. Not without telling Matt why I need him. "He's going to kill me, Matt."

"I don't care." His flat words gut me. I did wrong, but I'm still a person. I don't deserve to die.

"You should." I meet his eyes, steeling my spine. "Because I'm pregnant... and it's yours."

The look on his face would be comical, except I'm in a fight for my life—and my child's—right now.

He stares at me as the words sink in. Then his mouth curls into a sneer. "The fuck are you talking about?"

"I'm pregnant," I repeat.

He hauls me out of the room, and I don't fight him this time. I'm feeling weak, light-headed. I need to sleep, to rest after my hospital admission. The doc told me to take it easy. She didn't mention anything about being dragged around by a biker.

When we're in the corridor, he pushes me against the wall, his hand wrapping around my throat.

"You want to run that by me again?"

"Let go of me first," I grind out.

He looks like he's going to deny my request, but then he loosens his hold and steps back. His hands go into his jeans pockets, as if he needs to put them somewhere before he attacks me again.

I rub at my throat, swallowing down bile. "I'm sorry for what I did. I was desperate."

"I don't give two fucks about the money, Elyse—if that is even your name."

"Elyse is my name. Elyse Taylor." I blow out a breath, wondering how to explain this to him. "My dad is a deadbeat prick who ran up huge gambling debts and disappeared one night, leaving me to pick up the pieces."

"If you're trying to make me feel sorry for you, this ain't fucking working, babe."

"I'm not. I'm just explaining why I stole that money."

The intensity in his gaze scares me, and it's almost a relief when his eyes lower to my stomach. "It's definitely mine?"

"Yes, it's fucking yours. I wouldn't be here if it wasn't." I rile at his question. Does he think I make a habit of fucking strangers?

"I used a condom."

"From when? Nineteen-ninety-five?"

He scowls at my sarcastic tone. "It was fucking new."

"So? Condoms fail, Matt." My vision rolls. I stumble and he grabs me by the biceps, steadying me.

"What's wrong?" he demands.

"What do you care?"

"I don't." His words gore me. I didn't expect Matt to drop to his knees and hug my stomach, but it didn't expect such indifference to knowing his child is growing inside me.

It hurts more than it should.

I'm so tired. I just want to sleep. "I don't have the energy to argue with you."

"So why'd you fucking come here?"

"For help."

"Because someone is trying to kill you? Babe, you'll have to do better than that."

He doesn't believe me…

"You think I'm lying?" I gasp when he leans into me, his teeth bared.

"I think you don't want me to follow through on my threat and you'd say anything to stop me. You've already manipulated me once, Elyse. You made me believe we had a fucking connection. You used your body to fool me, then you stole from me."

"I needed the money—"

"Well now you've got ten grand towards taking care of your fucking kid. If there even is a fucking kid."

His words floor me. "Why I would I lie about being pregnant?"

"Honestly, I don't have a clue what goes on in your warped little mind. For all I know, you're using a fake pregnancy to get more fucking money off me. I'm not playing this game. Get fucking gone."

He strides back through the double doors, leaving me standing there—alone. I stare at the doors for a moment, hoping he'll step through them. When he doesn't, I turn and leave the clubhouse.

As I step back onto the street, I feel terror clutching my heart. I'm in so much trouble.

I walk home. I don't have enough money for the bus. By the time I get back to my flat, I'm running on fumes.

That's why I don't see Howard waiting out front of the building. Not until I'm nearly on top of him.

"W-what are you doing here? It's not been a month yet."

"No, but my cock was feeling fucking lonely." He smirks. "Let's go inside."

He grabs my arm and steers me inside the building. I have no choice but to follow him.

"You can't do this," I hiss at him as I try to pull free from his grip. My skin prickles as I realise how screwed I am.

"Until you pay that fucking debt back, I own you and your pussy. I can do whatever the fuck I want to."

He drags me up the stairs. Fear for me, for my baby, overwhelms me. I kick out, fighting every step. He is stronger than me, and I'm so weak, so tired, I barely hurt him.

At the front door, he pauses. "Keys."

I don't give them to him, but that doesn't deter him. He rummages in my pockets and finds them. He keeps his grip on me as he pushes the door open. My heart races as he kicks the door shut behind him.

Within a beat, he has me pressed against the wall, his hand wrapped around my throat. I can hardly breathe past his grip. Dark spots start to spill across my vision. I have to fight or I'm dead.

Somehow, I find the strength to knee him in the balls. I put everything I have into it. He lets go of me and I suck a breath in. I rush towards the door, but he fists his fingers into my hair and drags me back. I stumble, my knees connecting with the floor hard enough to jar my bones. He kicks out, hitting my side. I try to curl into myself to protect my stomach, to protect my baby.

"No!" I blurt as he smashes his fist into my face.

Pain erupts through my face, the skin tightening instantly over my cheekbone.

He barely gives me time to recover before he drags me up and walks me over to the sofa, which is set up as my bed. My feet scrabble in an attempt to dig in, but I'm no match for his brute strength and determination.

I'm really dizzy, and my head feels foggy as he shoves me down onto the sofa. Instantly, I try to squeeze my thighs together, but his knee goes between my legs, stopping them from closing.

He's going to rape me.

He's going to fuck me on my own bed.

No.

This isn't happening.

I bite his hand as it comes close to my face, tearing at the skin. My mouth fills with blood as I pierce it.

He roars, and I see him clench his fist before he slams it into my face. My head snaps to the side, my brain ringing. I gasp out a breath, barely getting it out before he punches me again.

"Stop fucking struggling!" he hisses.

I've been afraid in the past, but this is something else. I can't breathe through the fear as he holds my hands over my head, clamping them in place.

"Howard, stop," I gasp as he uses his free hand to pull my jeans down. His fingers push roughly inside me. It burns so badly I whimper.

"You owe me, bitch. I say suck my cock, your only answer is to get on your knees. I want to fuck you, you spread your whore legs and let me inside you."

He keeps his hold on my hands but pulls his fingers out of me so he can pull his jeans down.

This is happening. I can't stop it. I can't fight him. He's too strong. I just have to survive it. Just get through it. I close my eyes and brace as I feel him push against my entrance.

I catch movement behind him. Aaron.

He slams something against Howard's head. He blinks and then sags to the side.

Aaron's breathing hard as he stares at the collapsed body.

"Fuck," he mutters.

I don't chastise him for his language. I've never been so glad to see him as I am in this moment.

"We… we need to get out of here… before he comes to," I say.

I pull my underwear back up, my jeans too. Shame burns through my face that my brother is seeing me like this, but Aaron's peering down at Howard.

I get up on shaky legs and go to my brother. I grab his face, pulling his attention back to me. "We need to go."

"Are you… are you okay? Did he… was he trying to…?"

A sick look crosses his face, and I hate that he even has to ask the question. I shake my head. "I'm fine."

"You're not. You're bleeding."

I reach up and touch where his eyes are focussed. My fingers come away sticky with blood.

Shit.

I wince. It'll have to wait.

"Come on," I say, pulling Aaron out of the flat. I close the door behind us, making sure the lock clicks. I don't know how long we have until Howard comes to, but I don't want to be anywhere near him when that happens.

"Quickly," I say as I usher him down the stairs. "Why

aren't you in school?" I ask as we reach the bottom step and push through the door that leads onto the street.

"School finished an hour ago, Elyse."

I start moving up the street, my grip on my brother's arm. Where is safe? We can't go home. Matt made it clear he didn't believe me. He's the only chance we have though. I don't have money. I don't even have my purse with me.

"Do you have any money on you?" I ask Aaron.

"Yeah. I've got my bus fare for school and lunch money."

I hate taking it off him, but there's no way he's going to school anyway. Not with an irate Howard out there. "Enough for a cab to Ancoats?"

He nods. "What's in Ancoats?"

"Help," I say, and I hope like hell that's true.

My last hope lies with a man who thinks I'm lying about being pregnant and told me less than an hour ago to leave him the fuck alone.

But what other choice do I have?

I can't fight Howard alone, and when Matt realises I am pregnant, he will change his tune. I'm sure of it.

I hold on to that hope, because right now, hope is all I have left.

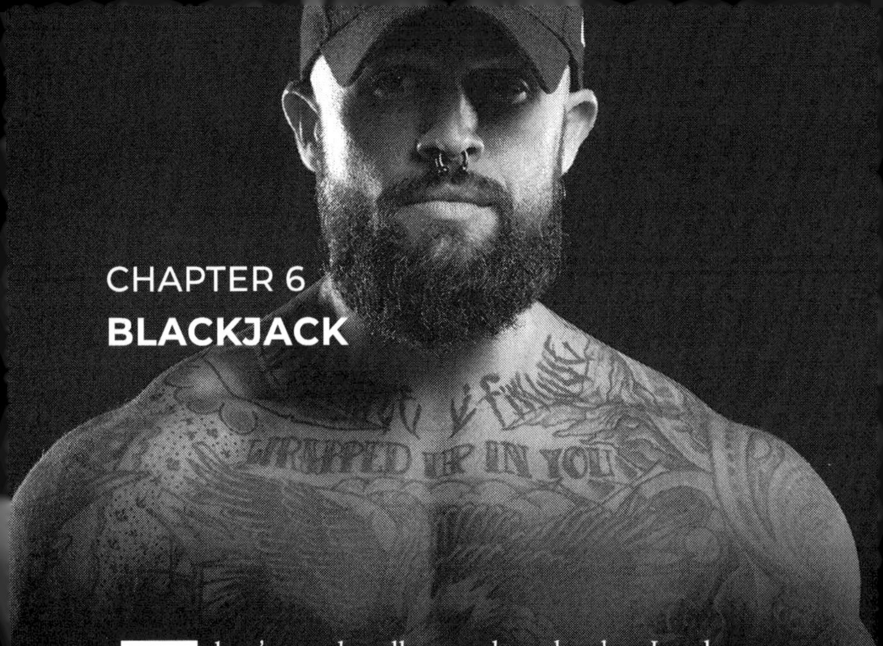

CHAPTER 6
BLACKJACK

Elyse's words roll around my head as I make my way back into the common room. Howler is on his feet, standing at the bar. He comes to me, meeting me in the middle of the room.

"You want to explain the crazy redhead?"

I really don't, but I step around Howler and go to the bar. I pick up the stool I knocked down and sit on it. Howler joins me.

"She's some bitch I met in the casino," I say. Fuck, I don't want to admit she fleeced me, but this is Howler. I tell this fucker everything. "We fucked and then she robbed me."

Howler arches a brow. "You let that tiny slip of a girl rob you?"

"Don't fucking start," I grumble. "That shit has come between me and my sleep since it happened. I let her leave with the money. I don't have the first fucking clue why, but I just… let her go."

"You're getting soft in your old age," Howler jokes. I smack him in the gut.

"Ain't anything fucking soft about me, cunt."

He smirks then turns serious. "The baby yours?"

"I don't know that I even believe there is a fucking baby. Every word out of her mouth to me from the moment I laid eyes on her has been a lie. Why would this be any different?"

"So make her do a test. If that's your kid—"

He breaks off with a shrug. He doesn't need to say the words. I grew up in a shit home. My father was a piece of crap, and my mother drank more than she parented. That was why I found the army. I had nothing else. No money, no prospects. I enrolled at eighteen and did four years before I'd had enough of the routine and rules. I liked the sense of brotherhood, but I fucking hated the regimented nature of the army.

I found the club soon after.

Ravage wasn't president then, but the former Sons London prez saw potential in me. I was twenty-two, angry and listless. The club gave me purpose.

Howler was a patched member when I prospected, but he was the brother I was closest to from the moment I stepped into that clubhouse. When Rav asked him to come to Manchester to set up a new chapter, there was no way I was staying behind and letting him go alone.

"You'd be happy if Pia got pregnant?" I ask.

"Fuck yeah, but I want a little more time with her before we start thinking of babies. She still has a lot of healing to do—from the abuse and with her parents. Wouldn't be the right time."

Socket steps into the room. Fuck, with everything going on, I forgot he is marrying Valentina this afternoon in a small ceremony. Only Pia and Howler are attending.

I whistle and he rolls his eyes, but the brother scrubs up well. He's wearing black jeans, a dress shirt and his kutte.

"Everything sorted for tonight?" he asks Howler. There will be a party back at the clubhouse tonight for everyone to celebrate. Considering my day, the last thing I want to do is party, but this is important, and Socket is a brother. I'll be here for him.

"I've sent some of the bunnies to get shit for it."

He nods, and I can see the nerves running through him.

"Never seen you in a shirt, brother," I say around a smirk.

Socket tugs at the collar. "This shit is strangling me. Feels like a fucking straitjacket. How do pricks wear this crap all the time?" He glances around the room. "Where's Pia?" he asks, a hint of concern in his voice.

"Don't worry, brother. She's coming."

I guess there must have been a worry Pia wouldn't go to see her parents marry.

"There's still time to run," I joke, trying to lighten the mood.

"Fuck no. Valentina is it for me." He gets a weird look on his face, almost dreamy. I've seen the brother stab men, gut them, covered in blood. This shit has me cocking my brow.

"You need a minute?" I ask.

He punches me in the gut. "One day, you'll find your old lady, and you'll see," he warns. "She'll fucking crash through your life and turn it upside down, and you won't give a fuck as long as she's with you."

I snort. Fucking doubtful.

"He's got enough fucking problems right now," Howler says.

"The redhead?" he guesses.

"You leave me to worry about her. Focus on getting married."

Socket pats my chest. "Good luck, brother."

I leave them sorting shit out and head out to the garden, the cooler air a relief.

Fucking Elyse.

I don't know what to believe, or what to do for that matter.

She seemed genuinely fucking terrified of whatever was going on in her life, but then she's played me in the past. This could also be a ploy to get more money from me. Pretend she's in trouble, tell me she's pregnant, and hope I'll do anything to protect her and that baby.

It seems convenient fucking timing. I'm guessing she's blown through that ten grand already.

I pull out a packet of cigarettes and light one. I don't smoke often, but right now I need to take the edge off. My leg jiggles as I get that first hit of nicotine. Fuck. I need to clear my head. That means I need to ride. It's the only fucking thing that helps when my brain feels scattered like this.

I stub my smoke out and make my way back through the clubhouse. I don't see Socket or Howler in the common room, so I guess they've headed to the registry office. I continue through the building, until I step out onto the street.

It's quiet, as it usually is. Rows of bikes are parked in front of the clubhouse, shimmering in the mid-afternoon sunlight.

As I walk over to my bike, the tension in my shoulders is already starting to loosen a little. Not surprising. My motorcycle is a thing of beauty. I've had her just over six months. Brand new off the forecourt—paid for with casino winnings.

I run a hand over the chrome engine and reach for my helmet.

A car pulling into the street catches my attention. There's no through route, so traffic is pretty much non-existent down here. It's unusual enough that it makes me stop what I'm doing. It's a taxi.

I watch as the back door opens, and a kid gets out. He's got floppy hair that he keeps shoving out of his face as he helps someone out. Flaming red hair is all I register at first. Then I realise who the fuck it is.

Elyse.

There's blood on her swelling face.

Rage races through my blood as my feet move before I can stop them. In a few strides, I'm in front of the kid and Elyse.

"The fuck happened?" I demand. The kid steps between us, glaring up at me.

"Who the hell is this guy, Elyse? Why are we here?"

"He's going to help." Elyse peers up at me, and I see relief flash in her eyes. I've seen that look before, when I was in the army. She's looking at me like I'm her saviour. I'm not sure how that makes me feel. "Right?"

Her eyes turn heavy, and I just manage to grab her arms as she sags into me. Fuck. I don't expect to have her full dead weight so my knees buckle a little before I manage to keep her upright.

I brush her hair back off her face as I grip her, but her eyes are closed and her head lolls.

There's no moment of doubt or hesitation as I scoop her into my arms bridal-style.

"Where are you taking her?" the kid asks, sounding a little hysterical.

"Inside. Follow me."

Carrying Elyse like precious cargo, I walk back into the clubhouse, the kid on my heels. As soon as I step into the common room, brothers crowd in.

I lower Elyse onto one of the beat-up sofas, my eyes skimming over her face. I don't know what happened to her, but the blood, the swelling cheek… I can guess.

She said someone wanted her dead. Was this done by whoever that person is?

I spot Trick in the crowd. "Can you get Mara here?" I ask.

He nods and steps away, his phone in his hand as he does. I turn to the kid.

"Name?"

He grinds his jaw, and I don't think he's going to answer. Then he says, "Aaron."

"How do you know Elyse?"

"She's my sister."

I glance between them, and now that he's said it, I do see a familial similarity, but she's older than him by maybe a decade. He's got the same shaped nose, the same colour eyes, though his hair is not red like Elyse's. It's dark.

"What happened?" He doesn't answer. "Aaron, I need some fucking answers here."

"He was..." He breaks off, glancing away, his jaw tightening.

"Who was doing what?"

"He was trying to *rape* her."

It takes my brain a second to register his words. When I do, red films my vision. The fuck? Anger blazes through me, uncontrollable rage. I want to kill someone. The thought of some cunt taking from her what I've tasted makes me flame white hot.

I grab the kid by his jacket, fisting my fingers into the material. "You got three seconds to start talking. I want to know fucking everything."

Aaron doesn't look scared. He meets my frustration without flinching.

"Matt..." Elyse's breathy voice has my gaze snapping back to her. Her eyes are heavy but opening. Her fingers skim over her swelling cheek before she winces. "Leave him alone."

"I want answers," I tell her.

Her eyes move around the crowd. "I'll tell you. But not here."

I huff out a breath and lift her again. There's barely anything of her, and for some reason that pisses me off. If she is pregnant, she needs to eat better.

If…

I don't want to be so mistrustful, but she hasn't exactly given me reason to put my faith in her.

I carry her across the hallway and into one of the rooms that is set up as a bedroom. It's used mostly by bunnies and out of towners. I don't lie her on the bed. No doubt that's a petri-dish of DNA. Instead, I place her on the sofa against the wall.

Aaron shoves past me and kneels at his sister's side. "Why are we here, Elyse?"

Her eyes come to me. "Because we need help."

"Babe, I already told you I ain't playing games with you."

She tries to sit up, but as she struggles, I find my hand pressing against her shoulder, pushing her back down. She gives up almost instantly, and I can see how weak she is.

That concerns me.

"I know you don't think very much of me, Matt, but I don't know where else to go." I try to ignore how the hurt in her voice makes me feel. "I'm scared, and I'm at the end of this road. I have nowhere left to turn."

"I don't trust you," I say.

She glances at her brother. "Can you wait outside? I need to talk to Matt alone."

Aaron's gaze slides from his sister to me. "I'm not leaving you with *him*."

She grabs his hand. "Matt won't hurt me. Please."

Her brother huffs a breath. "She'll be okay, kid," I assure him. "Go wait outside."

He glances between us, then pushes up to his feet and makes his way to the door. He gives his sister a final look before stepping out into the corridor.

As soon as we're alone, I turn back to her. "You want to tell me what the fuck is going on?"

I shouldn't care. She ain't my problem. This ain't my shit to deal with, but even without the possibility of my kid inside her, she draws me in, makes me want to fix things for her.

"I haven't lied to you about anything. Someone really is trying to hurt me." My eyes drop to the red marks on her neck. Finger marks.

My eyes narrow. "Who?"

She sighs. She looks fucking exhausted. Her eyes are ringed with black smudges. "His name's Howard. I don't know his last name, before you ask. My father ran up quarter of a million pounds worth of gambling debts with this man. He's some kind of loan shark from what I can gather. He gave the money to Dad and expected it back, with interest. The thing is, Dad isn't that good at gambling. He lost more than he won." Her smile is a little wobbly, and I can see the underlying pain as she talks. "He disappeared one day. I found Aaron alone, without food in the house, trying to survive. I brought him home with me and just thought Dad was doing his usual shit of vanishing without a bloody trace." She swallows hard, her throat working. "Then Howard turned up."

"The loan shark."

She nods. "At first, he just wanted small amounts. I could pay it from my wages. The amount kept increasing every month. It was beyond what I could manage. I got a second job to help, but the past few months he wanted tens of thousands paying back. Even if I worked ten jobs, I could never raise that amount of cash."

I take her explanation in. Howard… I've never heard that name, but it could be an alias.

"What happened today?"

"I already paid him for this month. Then he showed up, wanting…" She licks her lips. "More. I didn't have more. I never have what he asks for, but today was different."

"He tried to rape you."

Her gaze collides with mine, and I see the disgust on her face. "I fought him." Her hand goes to her stomach. "I couldn't let him do that to me. Not now."

That she's pregnant.

She doesn't say the words. She doesn't have to. I hear them loud and clear in my head.

"Fuck," I growl. "He manage to—?"

"No. Aaron stopped him. We left Howard unconscious on the living room floor, but he's going to be livid when he comes around. He'll kill us both." She grips my biceps. "I know I lied, and I know I played you, but I'm not lying about this. You're our only hope of survival."

I see something around her wrist as her sweater falls

down her arm. She notices my line of sight and tries to pull away.

I don't let her. It takes me a second to realise what it is. A hospital band.

"When were you in the hospital?" Elyse doesn't answer. She just tugs her sleeve over the band. "Elyse?"

My tone is hard, firm. She raises her eyes to meet mine. "Last night."

"For what reason?"

"I passed out at work. They called the paramedics, and I spent the night in accident and emergency."

"Why did you pass out?"

"The doc said it can happen in early pregnancy."

The knock on the door stops my reply, though in truth I'm not sure what I would have said. If she isn't pregnant, this is a long game to play, but if she is…?

That's my kid in her belly.

I want to know why the fuck she passed out.

I twist to look over my shoulder as Mara puts her head around the frame. Trick's old lady is small with a pixie haircut. She's not dressed like a doctor. She has a mini skirt and a band tee on. "Not interrupting, am I?"

I shake my head.

She steps fully into the room, carrying her equipment bag on her shoulder. I watch as she drops it on the floor and sits on the edge of the sofa next to Elyse.

"I'm just going to check some of these injuries over," Mara says softly as she grabs a pair of gloves from her kit and pulls them on. She starts to examine the gash to

Elyse's head, where most of the blood must have come from. It's stopped bleeding, but it looks ugly.

"This is already starting to close," she says after a few moments of probing.

"A lot of the blood is… his," Elyse says. "I bit him."

Mara cocks a brow. "Good for you. Though it looks like he still got a few hits in, despite that. I can't feel any breakages to your cheek. Were you hurt anywhere else?"

She shakes her head.

"She's pregnant," I say.

Mara's gaze shifts to me before going back to Elyse. "How many weeks?"

"Eight."

"Baby's probably well protected at this stage, but if you start cramping or bleeding, let me know."

"Do you have pregnancy tests in your kit?" Elyse asks.

Mara frowns. "You said you're pregnant. Why would you want to do a test?"

"Because he doesn't believe me."

I hate the way she fucking says it. Like I'm the arsehole in this situation. "You want to get into why I don't believe you?"

Elyse closes her eyes. "What I really want to do is sleep."

"I have a couple of test strips." Mara rummages in her bag and pulls out a sample jar. "Go pee and bring it back."

She swings her legs over the edge of the sofa before standing. Mara steadies her as she wobbles. "Are you dizzy?"

"A little. I just need a second."

My fingers itch to reach out and touch her, but I keep my arms folded over my chest to avoid the temptation.

Mara helps her to the bathroom at the back of the room, and when the door is shut, she steps back to me.

"The baby yours?" she asks.

There's no judgment in her words. "She says so. Timing would fit, but…" I shift my shoulders.

"You don't believe her?"

"We didn't exactly meet under the best of circumstances. She's done nothing but lie to me from the moment we met, so I'm finding it hard to trust a word that comes out of her mouth." I glance at the bathroom door. "She was in the hospital last night. Can you find out why?"

Mara drops her hands to her hips and huffs at me. "Here's a novel idea, Blackjack. Why don't you just ask her?"

"Because she'll say anything to get help from me. Ain't sure this isn't some elaborate plan to get money out of me."

"Has she asked for money?"

"Well, no."

"Just to play devil's advocate for a moment, Blackjack. If she is pregnant with your kid, what are you aiming for here? To be a father? To have her in your life?"

"If it's my kid, then hell yeah I want to be in its life."

"Maybe try to build some bridges then, rather than snarling."

"Ain't fucking snarling," I grind out.

"You're not exactly being friendly either." She drops a

hand to her hip, like a mother scolding a child. "I don't know what's going on, but put yourself in her shoes. She's clearly scared, alone, and has a baby inside her to protect."

The door opens and a pale Elyse is standing in the frame. She hands the sample jar to Mara, who goes to the chest of drawers to do the test.

"You okay?" I ask, Mara's words ringing through my head.

Elyse nods. "Help me back to the sofa." I don't walk her; I pick her up in my arms and carry her. "I could have walked with help," she grumbles.

"What's the point in you walking when I can carry you?"

I stand back from the sofa, peering down at Elyse. She looks delicate, nothing like she did that day in the casino. She's raw right now, wide open for me to see all her scars.

I don't like it.

It doesn't feel good to see her like this, no matter what I think of her.

"Well, it's positive," Mara says. "You are pregnant."

Elyse's tired eyes come to mine. "Now do you believe me?"

There's no denying the second line on the strip. It's there, clear as fucking day. She is pregnant. If she's eight weeks, that matches up with when we were together in the casino.

"I used a fucking condom," I mutter, feeling like this is some kind of fucking joke the universe is having at my expense.

"They can fail," Mara says in her best doctor voice.

I interlace my fingers at the nape of my neck. Anger, denial, and something else rolls through me. Something I can't quite put my finger on. Hope maybe?

"You're going to be a father," Elyse says, "and while I don't matter to you, I hope our child does."

It does, and that's the problem, because whatever trouble she's in, I'm going to have to fix.

Because nothing is touching my kid.

If I'm being honest, I'm not letting anything touch her again either.

"Fuck," I mutter.

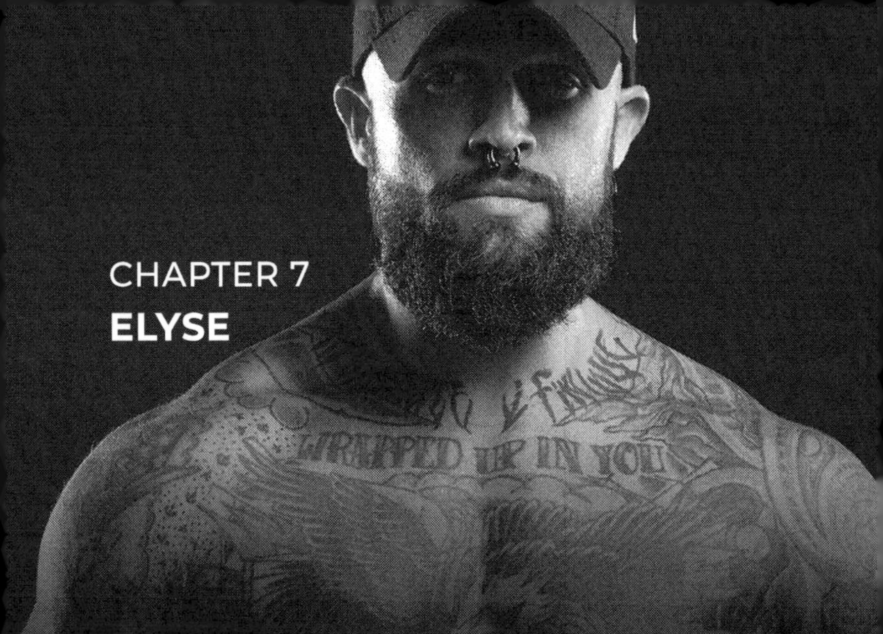

CHAPTER 7
ELYSE

I'm so tired. I could sleep for a week, but I keep my eyes firmly locked on the man in front of me. The man clearly losing his mind. It's a lot to digest. He's having a baby with someone who is pretty much a stranger.

I haven't really accepted it either, even though I've seen our baby on a screen, but we have to face reality. This baby exists. If he wants to be involved, I won't stop him, but if he doesn't…

That's his prerogative too.

I watch as the doctor packs up her kit. "If you need anything," she tells me, "tell one of the brothers to find Mara."

I nod, overwhelmed by her kindness.

She leaves the room, and the air grows tense between me and Matt. He's standing in front of the chest of drawers, staring down at the test strip. I wonder what's going through his head.

"I know this is hard," I say. "But I need to know where your head is at. I want to keep the baby, but Howard is still out there. If you won't help me and Aaron, I need to leave town, find somewhere safe."

I doubt anywhere safe exists from that bastard. I have no idea how we'll run either. I have no money, no savings. No means to get away, but we have to do something.

"You ain't leaving town. Not while my kid's in your fucking belly."

The vehemence in his voice makes a shiver run up my spine.

"I want my baby safe, Matt. That isn't here without your help."

He turns to face me, his expression unreadable.

"Our baby. If you ain't lying, it's mine too. I get a say in what happens to it. You try to leave town, I'll tie your arse to my fucking bed."

My brows crawl up my forehead as an ugly feeling washes through me.

"That's your plan here? To threaten me?" I ignore his statement questioning the paternity. I understand his hesitations, his doubts. I deserve his vitriol.

"If that's what keeps you here, then yeah." He leans into me, a dark look on his face. "You run, and I'll fucking find you. I won't let you take my child from me."

My chest starts to feel so tight I can't drag a breath in. It's like a plug is lodged in my throat. Have I made things worse by coming here? Not only do I have Howard on my trail, now I have Matt too. "That's not my plan. I want to stay, but I can't do this alone. Howard will hurt me."

"That cunt's not an issue." He waves this off as if it's nothing. He has no idea how dangerous Howard is.

"He's very much an issue," I counter. "He tried to rape me. He nearly succeeded too. If Aaron hadn't been there…" Pain lances through my chest as I let my brain reach for the worst-case scenario. That would have been something I would never come back from. Bad enough the other shit he's done to me, but that… that would be the final straw. "What do you think he's going to do to us both now? Aaron hurt him."

"You let me worry about that prick."

"Matt."

He gives me his attention. "Don't know who the fuck this guy is, Elyse. Never heard his name, so that means he ain't a big player in the city. I have my club and my brothers at my back, so when I tell you that you don't have to worry, I mean it. You and Aaron are staying here until we find Howard."

"And after that?"

"We don't have to be together to co-parent."

I'm surprised by the level of disappointment that hits me in the chest at his dismissal. "Right. Of course not. I just… I didn't mean with us."

"There is no us. There's you, there's me, and there's our kid. I'll do whatever it takes to look after my child, Elyse, but you and I aren't a thing and we're never going to be a thing. I don't fucking trust you, and I can't be with someone I don't trust. Get some rest. I'll be back soon."

He leaves the room. As soon as he does, I feel the tears

pricking my eyes. I wipe them quickly as Aaron steps inside.

"What did that dick do to you?" he demands as a tears streak down my cheeks, escaping before I can stop them.

"He didn't do anything. I messed up, Aaron."

I did. I screwed any chance me and Matt may have had of being together, of making us into a real family.

He glances towards the door before bringing his attention back to me. "Is he going to help us with Howard?"

I nod. "His club has resources to... I don't know? Stop him from retaliating." I grab Aaron's hand. "We'll be okay."

We just have to stay protected until he's out of the picture. Then, we can get back to normal—whatever that looks like. Custody agreements and weekend visits. Trying to raise a preteen who will be a teenager when the baby comes, and a newborn.

I stare up at the ceiling, trying not to fall apart at how overwhelmed I am. I'm exhausted, running on fumes. My body feels rung out like an old dish cloth, but I need to tell my brother everything.

"I need to tell you how I got that first ten grand for Howard."

He comes and sits on the edge of the sofa, so close to me he's nearly touching me. "You did something dodgy, didn't you?" There's no disappointment in his tone, but there is curiosity.

"I went to the casino in Ancoats. I watched and saw who was winning big." I don't want to tell him this, but he needs to hear it from me, not in anger off Matt. "I saw

Matt was doing well and I caught his eye. We… ended up in a hotel room together."

"You shagged?" He smirks as he says it.

I frown, not even wanting to know how he knows about shagging. "Yes," I admit. "In the morning, I left and stole his winning chips. He caught me."

Aaron's eyes flare. "Did he hurt you?"

I shake my head. "Matt's not like that."

"He's a biker, Elyse."

"What do you know about bikers?"

He shifts his shoulders. "I hear stuff."

Probably from Jordan. That kid is wild. I probably should discourage their friendship, but they've been friends since they were little.

"What have you heard?"

"That they're dangerous. They've murdered people."

I'd heard similar stories too. "Matt's angry because I took the money, but also because I'm… pregnant."

Aaron stares at me a beat before his eyes slide to my flat stomach. "Whoa."

"Yeah, kid. Whoa."

"Where's it going to sleep?"

It is a solid question. I'm already on the sofa in our flat. Aaron has the only bedroom. "I don't know."

"Do you want me to leave?"

For a moment, I don't compute what he said. When I do, my heart clenches. "No! Not even for a second have I considered you leaving, Aaron. Wherever I go, you go."

The relief that crosses his face makes me wonder where his head has been since we arrived at the Sons' clubhouse. "I don't want to be in the way. I know this isn't what you signed up for."

My heart shatters for him.

I grab his hand and squeeze it. "I'm not our father, Aaron. I'm not leaving you. I promise."

His eyes go back to my stomach. "Can I pick its name?"

I laugh. "No."

Aaron's nose wrinkles. "You suck."

"Yeah, get used to it."

A beat of silence passes between us. "Are we going to die?"

His words shock me. "What? Of course not. Why would you think that?" Even as I say this, I wonder how true it is. Matt's protection is all that stands between us and Howard's wrath. I'm relying on the fact Matt cares about our baby, but that could change at any moment.

Aaron shifts his shoulders. "Just seems like that might happen."

"No one is dying. Matt is going to take care of everything." I hope like hell that's true.

"How long are we staying here for?"

"I don't know."

He mulls this over. "Okay then." The resilience of children.

Aaron sits on the floor in front of the sofa, always my protector. He pulls his phone out and starts to play a game on it. I try to stay awake, but my eyes are heavy and I'm exhausted.

As I drift off, my last thought is: are we safe here?

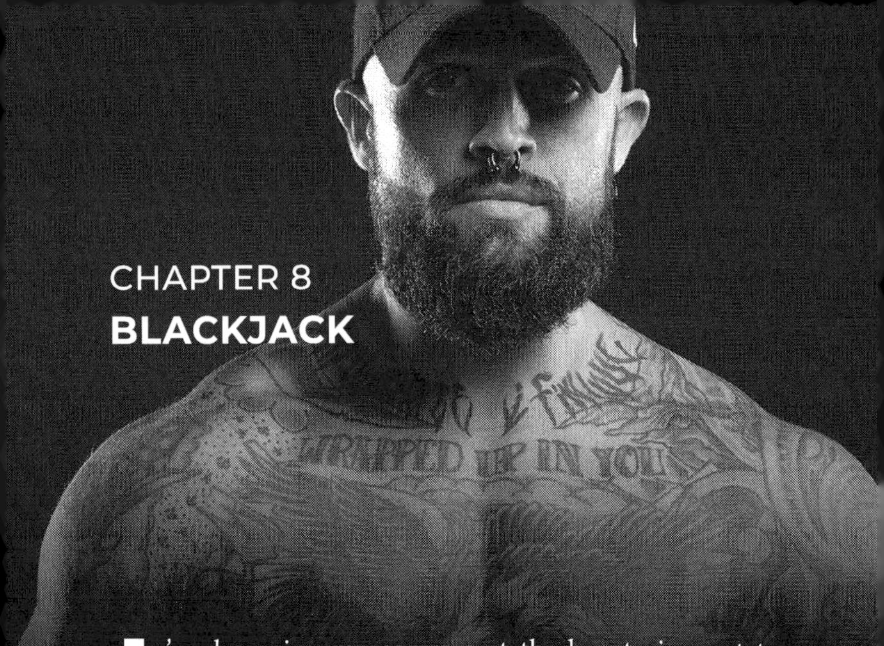

CHAPTER 8
BLACKJACK

I'm drowning my sorrows at the bar, trying not to think about the pretty little redhead across the hallway. More like a fucking Siren.

I push that thought down as soon as it enters my head. She manipulated me, sure, but I know why now. I can understand why she did it, even if I don't like that she did.

What did you expect? Her to ask you nicely for the money?

I would have laughed in her face if she'd asked me for ten grand.

I would have laughed myself fucking sick.

There is no way in hell I would have handed over my winning chips, so stealing it was the only way for her to get it.

"I need to decorate the bar," Lissa says.

I glance over my shoulder at her. The room is decked out with banners, balloons and streamers ready for Valentina and Socket's return.

The last thing I want to celebrate is a wedding when my own love life is a dumpster fire.

"So decorate it," I mutter, lifting my glass and taking a swig. The alcohol burns as it slides down my throat.

"You're in the way."

"Bitch, you keep talking to me like that and you're going to find your arse outside the front doors."

I grab the bottle of Jack in front of me and pour another measure. Fuck her.

Lissa glares but knows better than to argue, so she walks off, muttering under her breath about how much of a prick I am. I can't even argue with that assessment. I am being a dick.

But all I can think about is the fact Elyse is pregnant.

And it's mine.

This Howard cunt is going to get a lesson he'll never forget. There had been real fear, total terror when she'd been talking about him coming for her. No one could fake it that well.

I spot Brewer. The brother is enthusiastically helping the bunnies get the room ready for the happy couple to return. I signal him over and wait while he puts down the streamer he was about to pin to the wall and comes to me.

Brew is our treasurer. He has thick red hair, no beard, but tattoos running up his neck. At thirty-seven, he's five years older than me, and he's always been a solid addition to the club.

He's a good brother.

One I trust.

He's also personable, which means he knows a lot of fuckers.

"You done snarling at the girls?" he asks with a smirk. I ignore that.

"You heard of a loan shark who goes by the name of Howard?"

He thinks for a moment. "Not heard the name before, but that isn't to say he isn't operating in the city. Since we shook shit up, a lot of smaller thugs have been trying to carve a path. Why?"

We'd shook shit up that much we pushed most of the major threats to us out of the city centre of Manchester and into the suburbs. A ring of enemies surrounding our kingdom. We'd done enough to keep them down, and we'd put down any threat fast. I would have preferred to run everyone out of town, but in a city the size of Manchester and its suburbs, that is never going to happen.

Either way, the streets ran with blood by the time we were done. We carved out our territory, and our enemies will have to pry it out of our dead fucking hands.

I stood at Howler's side the entire time. His right-hand man. I would die for my brother. For any of my brothers. We are family, even if it ain't in the traditional sense.

"I think that's who Elyse is tied up with," I say.

"The redhead?" He waggles his eyebrows.

"Yeah."

"She's fucking cute. Can see why you like her. Little young for you, though, isn't she?"

I smack him in the gut. I'm at least a decade older than her but I don't need reminding of the fucking fact.

"I fucked her once. Saw her in the casino. Couldn't fucking resist her," I admit.

"I heard what she said. She's pregnant. Should I be congratulating you or commiserating?"

"Ain't sure on that front yet, brother. That's going to take a hell of a lot of time to work through. Never expected to be a dad, and not with a woman I fucked once."

"Do I need to talk to you about safe sex?"

I roll my eyes. "I can't believe I'm even fucking saying this, but I wrapped. Don't know how it happened, but that condom was good."

Brew shifts his shoulders. "I know plenty of kids who exist because of birth control failures. Question now is: what are you going to do?"

"Raise my fucking kid," I snap at him. "What the fuck do you think I'm going to do?"

He raises his hands in defence. "Didn't mean to offend."

"The baby ain't the issue," I mutter. "It's this fucking loan shark. I can't have that fucker on Elyse's heels." I take a sip of my drink. I can't, and I won't. "I'll do whatever it takes to protect my kid, Brew, but I need to know what I'm dealing with here. She hasn't given me much to go on. This cunt is the type of fucker who uses sex in place of payment. He's a real fucking scumbag."

His eyes find mine. "That what he's been doing to your girl?"

Your girl...

Fuck, that phrase, for some reason, hits me in the chest. She ain't mine, but the ownership Brew placed on her by calling her that does something to me. It makes me want to claim her. She's got my child in her belly, and while I've never thought about kids, now I have one on the horizon I'm feeling protective as fuck.

"She says he tried to rape her," I say around a grimace. "Her brother stopped him, but the way he did, it's going to have repercussions. I want to make sure nothing comes back on her."

"I'll do some digging around, see if I can figure out who he is," Brew tells me.

"Thanks, brother."

"You want me to talk to my sister about the other thing?"

"The other thing?"

"The kid that's coming your way. She has four little crotch goblins. She might be able to offer some advice."

I snort at the crotch goblins. He fucking loves his nieces and nephews so there's no malice in the description.

"Yeah, that would be good," I say. "I have no fucking clue what to expect."

"Expect your life to be turned upside down," he says, clasping my shoulder. He wanders back off to help decorate, leaving me still sitting at the bar.

I glance in the direction of the doors. She's just on the other side of that corridor. I shouldn't want to go to her, but a little buzzed, I find myself pushing to my feet.

I want to see her.

I don't know why either, but the need grows inside me, festering.

When I step out into the corridor, I pause before the door. I can't hear sounds on the other side.

Not bothering to knock, I push into the room. Aaron, who is sitting in front of the sofa like a guard dog, comes to his feet instantly. His mouth pulling into a hard line as he takes me in. The kid is fearless. I like that.

My eyes drift from him to Elyse. She's lying on the sofa, her head twisted to the side. Her eyes are closed, and the rings beneath them look darker.

There's a towel from the bathroom covering her. I frown.

"You want a blanket, kid, you just have to ask."

"We're used to making do with what we have," he says with a shift of his shoulders. His hair is too long and keeps falling in his eyes, meaning he's constantly scraping it back.

I move over to the chest of drawers and open the bottom one. I pull out a throw and hand it to Aaron. He takes it suspiciously, and then covers his sister up. The care he shows as he tucks it around her makes my throat tighten. He loves her, respects her. It's clear to see from his attention.

"She's not as tough as she makes out, you know?" he says, continuing to fuss with the blanket. "She acts like she's made of steel, but she's scared. We both are."

"Nothing's going to touch either of you now," I promise.

It doesn't gall me to give that assurance, and it's not a lie either. I will protect her and Aaron.

Why?

That's a little more complicated to answer. It's getting harder to see Elyse as anything but a victim of her circumstances.

Aaron's gaze snaps to me. "Don't say that unless you mean it. People always let Elyse down."

"I mean it, kid. Your sister is having my kid. She ain't going anywhere without my fucking protection." I mean it too. That kid inside her is the most important thing in my life right now.

"How long has your father been in the wind?"

He grits his teeth together. "That prick." Aaron straightens and faces me. "He screwed Elyse. Left her to pick up the pieces of his mess. She's doing her best, but it's never enough. People always want more of her. Don't be like those dicks."

It's a warning to treat his sister well. "Elyse tell you how we met?"

"Yeah. She's having your kid." He eyeballs me like it's my fault.

"That's what she tells me."

"You don't believe her?"

"Didn't say that."

He snorts. "You didn't have to. I can hear it in your voice. My sister is a good person. She's done things to survive."

"I'm not doubting that, Aaron."

"Howard's a psycho. He would have really hurt her if I

hadn't been there."

"Tell me what you know about him."

"Just that our dad owed him money. He gambled. Horses, I think. He disappeared out of the blue. Came home from school and he was just gone. Elyse saved me. She brought me home with her and took care of me."

He cares about his sister. Deeply.

I can see it in the passion with which he talks about her.

"Do you know a last name?"

"Howard's? No. She always made me leave the flat when he came over."

"How often did he come over?"

"Every month. That's why him coming today didn't make sense. He only just came over."

"Your sister ever have the money to give him?"

He shakes his head. "Even when she got the ten grand from, um, you… it wasn't enough. She was short. He knows we can't pay it. Elyse works two jobs, but it'd never be enough. I wanted to get a weekend gig, but she wouldn't let me. Wants me focused on school, but school's boring."

That makes me think Howard's interest in Elyse isn't about the money—at least not completely. He knows she can't ever repay his debt.

So why is he doing this?

He wants *her*.

He wants to control and own her.

Was his attempted rape this time a one off? Has it happened before?

Possessiveness washes through me in a tidal wave. I push down my emotions and attempt to keep my expression impassive.

"He hurt Elyse before?"

He shakes his head. "Not like this."

I peer down at Elyse, who hasn't stirred since I came into the room. Her face is starting to blacken, and the swelling looks worse. It makes me want to put my fist through something.

"Why don't you go and hang out in the common room for a little bit? We're about to have a party. There's food."

His brows cock. "A party?"

"One of the brothers is getting married." I glance down at my watch. "They should be back by now."

Aaron glances at his sister before bringing his attention back to me. "I'm not leaving her."

"Understand that you feel that way, but you need to take care of yourself too. She needs you to be strong, kid."

He shakes his head. "She's not who you think she is. Keep that in mind." He moves to the door, pausing before he steps through it. "You hurt her, I'll hurt you."

With that threat, he steps through the door.

I shake my head. The balls on that kid.

I give my attention back to Elyse. She looks so frigging delicate lying there, bruised, but not broken.

Strong.

My gaze slides to her stomach. There's no indication of a baby bump yet beneath her hoodie, but I can't stop from imagining how she'll look with one. I can't stop myself. I sink onto the edge of the sofa and splay my hand out over her abdomen, trying to find any hint of a belly beneath my palm, but all I can feel is her flat stomach.

"Matt?" Her soft voice has my eyes sliding towards her. I don't move my hand, and she glances at it before returning her attention to me. A small smile crosses her face, and fuck, do I like it. I shouldn't, but I do. "You can't feel anything yet," she says, telling me what I already know. The kid is too small.

She places her hand over mine, so that we're both holding her stomach. I don't move, too scared to break through this moment we're having.

"Where's Aaron?"

"I sent him to the common room to get some food."

Warmth floods her eyes at my statement. "Thank you for taking care of him." She glances down at our joined hands. "I know this isn't how it's supposed to be, but I already love our baby," she says.

Fuck.

The emotions that roll through me make my breath catch in my throat.

"I promise you I ain't letting anything touch you or our kid."

Her smile does funny shit to me, but it's the hint of sadness in her eyes that makes me want to raze the world for her. "I hope that's the case, but Howard is powerful, Matt, and he wants to hurt me."

"He's not powerful. He's a cockroach who preys on those who can't fight back, and he's going to find out what my club does to cockroaches."

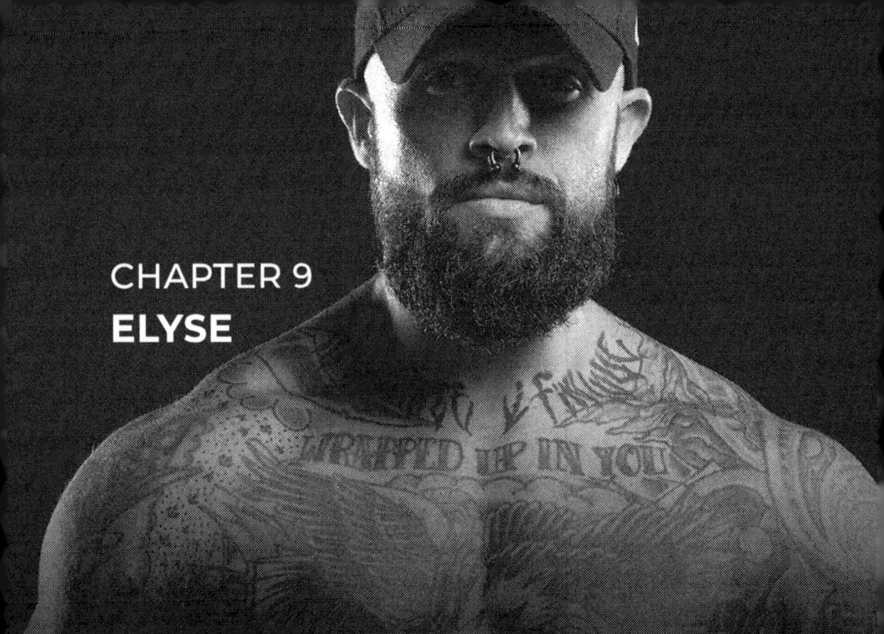

CHAPTER 9
ELYSE

I wish he'd tell me what is going through his head. Trying to read that impassive expression is driving me insane. He doesn't let a single emotion slide onto his face, but he doesn't move his hand from my stomach either. He looks so big perched on the edge of the sofa. I want to move, to give him more room, but I'm scared of stopping this moment between us.

"You're moving in with me," he says after a moment of silence.

His words surprise me. "What?"

"Need you somewhere I can protect you. Can't do that at your flat."

"I know but…moving in together is a big step, Matt."

"And having a baby isn't?" I don't miss the sarcasm laced in his words.

"Just because we're having a baby together doesn't mean anything has to change."

"You really think things can go back to how they were?" he asks.

"Well… not entirely. Of course not. But it doesn't mean we need to rush things."

"There's a lunatic rapist out there who wants to probably kill you and your brother. You think I'm just going to pat you on the arse and send you out into the world alone?" I don't, but moving in together? That's a huge step. "Don't read more into it than it is, Elyse. I need you close so I can keep you safe. That's all."

This dismissal stings more than it should. I pull my hand off his, unable to stop the hurt from rolling through me. Just when I think we're taking a step forward, we end up moving two back. Tears spring in my eyes of their own accord. Fuck. I'm going to cry. It's the last thing I want to do. He doesn't owe me anything—not even to be nice to me—and I don't want to guilt him with tears.

"Okay." I pull my bottom lip between my teeth to stop it from wobbling, glancing away so he won't see my tears.

"Are you… are you crying?"

I swipe angrily at my cheeks, annoyed at myself. "It's pregnancy hormones," I say, though I don't think that's the whole reason I'm upset.

He leans forward and uses his thumb to capture the tears rolling down my face. It's such a gentle gesture, so kind, it makes me cry more.

"Fuck. Shift over," he mutters.

I frown at him. "What?"

"Move over," he repeats.

Not understanding, I do as he asks anyway, scooting

deeper against the back cushions of the sofa, leaving a space on the edge. He stands and turns, putting his arse next to my body. Then he swings his legs up. Without warning, he pulls me against him. I stiffen for a moment. What is he doing?

His arms wrap around me, pulling me closer to his chest. He smells so good, and when I relax my face against him, the leather of his vest is soft on my skin. "This shit is hard," he says. It's not an apology, but I hear one in his words anyway.

"I know."

"We're both finding our way here, Elyse. It's going to take time."

"I know that too," I tell him.

"Don't want to make you fucking cry."

I laugh a little, the sound dry and without much humour. "I'd get used to it. I expect there will be more tears before the end of this pregnancy."

"I don't know what the fuck to do," he admits.

I wrap my arm around his waist, enabling me to snuggle deeper against his side. This feels good. Too good. I try not to let my imagination run away with itself. "Me neither. This is my first time being pregnant too," I tell him.

We sit in silence for a moment, just holding each other. We're in uncharted waters. Neither of us knows how to navigate it. This is terrifying. I don't know how to be a mother, how to take care of a baby.

"What if we suck at this?" I ask, a frightened timbre to my voice.

"You're already being a parent to Aaron and that kid is great."

"He wasn't at first. He was angry after Dad left him. So angry."

"He took that out on you?"

I shift my shoulders. "He had no one else he could take it out on. I was his only outlet. Over time we found our way, but it wasn't always easy."

"That kid worships you," I tell her.

"Until I force him to sit down and do his homework."

"There's a hell of an age gap between you."

"We only share a father. His mum left when he was a baby. Disappeared just like our dad. He's used to people leaving. I don't want to do that to him, ever. I'm the only constant he's got."

"You're a good sister. Not many twenty-year-olds would take on a younger sibling like that."

I don't correct him on the fact I'm twenty-two, not twenty.

"I couldn't abandon him. Not when everyone else in his life did that."

"You guys are going to need shit," he says, the sudden change of direction making me frown.

"What do you mean?"

"I want to make sure Howard's gone from your place, but you guys need stuff as well from home. I'll head over and pick up what you need. Make me a list."

My frown deepens. "I don't want you going there alone, Matt. I know you think you're invincible, but

Howard is dangerous. He's not going to play nice if you turn up and he's still there."

"I'll take back up with me."

It helps a little, but it doesn't calm the nerves running through me. "But—"

He speaks before I can protest. "No buts. I need to make sure that cunt is gone."

I don't want him to go, but I also know I can't stop him. "Okay. I'll make a list."

"Not the whole flat either. Just the shit you and Aaron can't live without."

I nod. That'll be easy. Neither of us has a lot of stuff anyway. I was already living on the poverty line when I took my brother in.

"We're having a party this afternoon," he says. "You should come. Relax a little, get to know the other club brothers and old ladies."

"I'm not sure that's a good idea," I say.

"It'll do you good to relax, unwind a bit. Stress ain't good for you, or the kid."

His concern makes me smile. "I know."

"Why don't you get cleaned up and I'll find you a clean sweater. I've got some shit stashed at the clubhouse for when I need a change of clothes."

My eyes snap to his face. I know his club has a reputation… one that is bloody, dark and violent.

My thoughts must show on my face because he snorts. "It rains in Manchester. Constantly. The clothes are for when I get wet on the back of the bike."

"Oh," I breathe out the word.

"Ain't saying I'm a good man, Elyse. I'm not. I've got blood on my hands, in my soul, but ain't a monster either."

"You would never have let me leave the hotel room that morning if you were a monster, Matt."

He shakes his head. "Still ain't sure why I did."

"Because you are a good man."

He grunts but doesn't answer. Instead, he swings his legs off the sofa and I'm forced to let him go. I hate that I am. I could have stayed clinched together like that for hours.

"Go and shower. I'll be back in a second with some clean stuff."

He stands and then holds his hands out to me. I take them, liking the strength of his touch and the way his palm scrapes over mine. Slowly, he helps me to my feet.

I don't wobble, but he keeps hold of me, as if he expects me to. "I'm okay," I assure him, because right now he seems like he needs it.

"Ain't sure you shouldn't be in the hospital right now, Elyse."

"Your doctor friend checked me over. I'm fine."

"She doesn't have one of those machine things that can see the baby, though."

"An ultrasound?"

"Yeah. I'd feel better if we could see him or her."

"I had an ultrasound at the hospital."

He snaps his head up to me. "And?"

"The baby was fine."

"You have a picture?"

"They didn't give me one. They had to do it inside me,

because the baby is so small." He looks disappointed. "I'll get another scan, Matt. You can come with me, if you'd like."

He mulls this over, then nods. "Yeah, I want to be there for all of it. Go and shower."

I make my way into the bathroom, locking the door behind me. It's clean, like the room, and there are some toiletries inside the shower cubicle. I twist the shower knob and wait as the water lets down. After a few minutes, steam starts to fill the room and I undress. I glance in the mirror, catching sight of my bruised face and neck. I have blood smeared down my face. It's a wonder they let us in the cab looking like this. I step under the spray and wash myself with some of the shower gel. It smells masculine, but as long as I'm clean, I don't care.

I wash my hair, even though I don't have the energy to.

I rinse the soap out after I've massaged it into my scalp, making sure the suds are totally gone. When I'm done, I switch the water off and step out of the shower. I grab a towel off the rack and wrap it around my body.

I take my time drying myself. Then I pull my underwear and jeans back on. I just need a clean top.

Wrapping the towel around myself, I slide the lock back and step cautiously back into the room. There's no sign of Matt, but there's a folded red garment on the bed. I move to it and pick it up, shaking it out. It's a hoodie, similar to the one I took off in the bathroom, but this has a zip up the front and a logo on the breast that I don't recognise. I drop the towel and slip it over my shoulders, before zipping it up.

I tie my wet hair into a ponytail, and then I leave the room.

I'm anxious to lay eyes on my brother, make sure he's okay. I hear the party before I push through the doors that lead into the bar area. Music is playing, some retro pop song I vaguely recognise but couldn't say the name of.

There's a woman standing in a white dress with a man in his forties who is wearing his vest with a white dress shirt. They are both smiling broadly.

There are a lot of people in the room, and it takes me a few moments to locate my brother, who is sitting in front of the buffet table with a plate full of food.

"You're awake," he says as I approach.

"You had enough to eat?"

He nods. "This food is amazing."

Guilt washes through me. We don't eat a lot of junk or treat food. There isn't the money to. I make meals that are cheap and go a long way.

"Don't make yourself sick," I warn.

He waves me off.

I feel a presence at my back. Matt. I turn as he steps up to me.

"Get some food." It sounds more like an order than a suggestion.

"I will in a moment," I tell him. "Thank you for the hoodie."

He eyes me, and I wonder what's going through his head as he takes me in. The look is appreciative.

"What?" I ask, wondering if I missed a spot of blood or something.

"You look good in my clothes," he says.

My cheeks heat, but he's turned to the table. He grabs a plate and hands it to me. "Eat, and try to have some fun."

He wanders away, leaving me standing there wondering what the hell just happened.

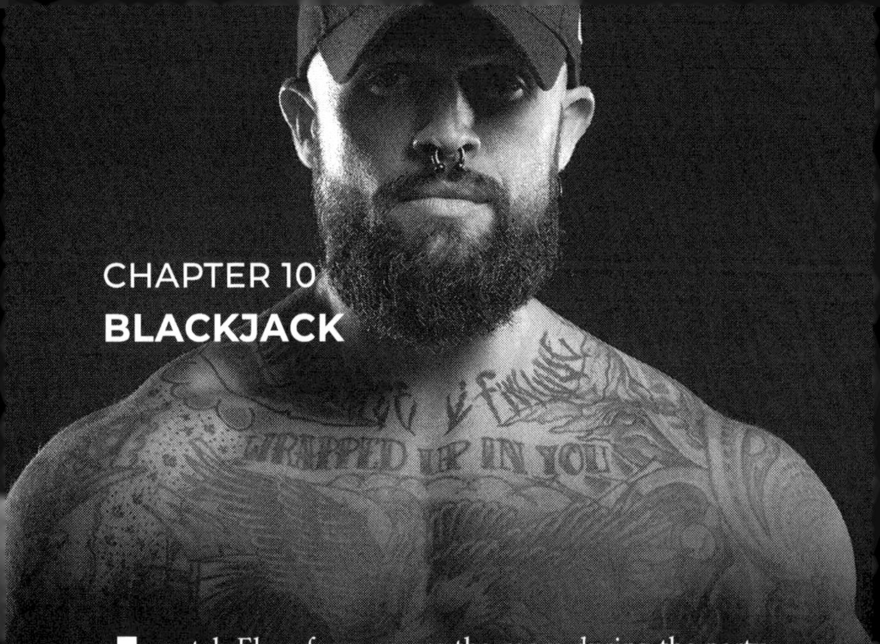

CHAPTER 10
BLACKJACK

I watch Elyse from across the room during the party. She isn't shy. She introduces herself to anyone she comes into contact with. Eventually, she settles on talking with Pia.

I can't keep my eyes off her. She's just as beautiful now as she was the night I saw her in the casino—even with the bruises and swelling.

Despite her nap, she still looks exhausted.

I want to put her back in bed and make her fucking rest. I want to get rid of those dark circles under her eyes.

I don't know why but I want to fix things for her.

"You could just go over and talk to her," Mara says, sliding in next to me and leaning her back against the bar. She's changed her clothes since she was here earlier and is wearing a short navy skater dress with black tights with little sunflowers on and a pair of Converse.

"Since when did you care so much about my relationships?" I ask without malice as I take a sip of my drink.

"Since it became the most interesting thing going on around here," she says, smiling.

"Don't you and Trick have enough excitement?"

"Trick and I are fine. Quit changing the subject."

"I don't do heart to fucking hearts, Mara." I keep my eyes locked on Elyse as she laughs at something Pia says to her. Fuck, it does something to me seeing her do that.

"None of you do. You're all as gruff as bears and twice as mean, but humour me, okay? I'm a person who likes to fix shit. It's why I became a doctor. Let me fix this."

I scowl at her, then huff out a breath. "I'm still pissed at her," I admit. "She stole from me. I don't take that lightly. I understand why she did it, but she still played me like an idiot."

"Ah, so it's pride standing in your way."

I shoot her a dark look. "Ain't pride and you know it."

She nods, tipping her bottle back to take a drink. When she lowers it, she says, "Being a stubborn arse isn't going to help either." I shoot her a glare, and she holds up a defensive hand. "Don't shoot the messenger. I'm just telling you what I see from the outside looking in. She's scared. She needs you, Blackjack, but you need to decide whether you want to be all in or not. You can't dance around it. You're having a baby together. That kid is going to need sane parents. Not like ours, right?"

I snort. Mara's parents were first-class narcissists. Mine were useless.

"I don't know the full story of what happened between you both, but I do know she was shaking when I examined her. Whatever happened to her, it left her terrified."

"Her dad ran off and left her paying a loan shark off."

She nearly chokes on her drink. "Shit."

"Yeah, shit," I mumble. "I know she took the money off me because she was desperate. I don't even give a shit about it. It was pocket change."

"Then what's the issue?"

"I don't trust her."

"A desperate person did a desperate thing. I don't think she's a career thief, Blackjack."

She's probably right about that. I never saw Elyse in the casino before the night we hooked up. If I was just a mark, she would have been there other times.

My eyes scan the room again, looking for Elyse, and I see her talking to Rug. He's a patched member, relatively new to the club. He's also a fucking whore who will shag anything with a heartbeat.

The way he's looking at my girl pisses me off.

Like he's got a chance.

Like she could be his.

He touches her arm, and she smiles at something he says.

I see red. I push up from the stool.

"Oh, come on, just indulge me a little longer. Blackjack!" Mara shouts after me as I cross the room, ignoring her, ignoring anything but the little fuck with his hands on my girl.

As I approach, Elyse's words trail off.

"Matt."

I ignore her and snag Rug by the front of his kutte, dragging him off his stool. "Off limits, dickhead."

He holds his hands up, as if pleading ignorance will help his cause. "We were just talking."

"Know for a fucking fact you were in the room when she turned up and told me she's carrying my kid, dickhead. Know you know that means she's not available for you to stick your tiny prick anywhere near her."

I shove him, and he stumbles back, tumbling over the table behind and sprawling onto the floor. I feel the attention of the room coming to me. I ignore it, blocking it out. Elyse is on her feet now, her face pale.

"Matt, stop."

I ignore her. I grab Rug off the floor, dragging him up, and slam him against the wall behind us. My fist balls and sinks into his gut. He lets out a grunt of pain and tries to push me back. I don't move. I have brawn on my side, and training. My army shit is like muscle memory. In comes back in a heartbeat, meaning I'm able to hit him where I know it will hurt.

We trade punches, him getting an uppercut to my gut while I hit him in the base of his jaw.

I can taste blood in my mouth, but no one moves to stop us. No one tries to intervene.

At least not one of our brothers.

"Stop!" Elyse grabs my arm and tries to haul me off him. It's that which stops me. I don't want her to get hurt.

I twist to glance over my shoulder. Her hand presses to her chest, as if she's trying to calm her throbbing heart.

I grab her arm. "We need to fucking talk," I mutter.

Aaron moves towards us, as if he's going to step between us, but his sister shakes her head.

She lets me drag her out of the room. I don't miss the look Howler gives me as I pass him, but I'll deal with him later. For now, I need to sort shit with Elyse.

I push her into the room she was in earlier and shut the door behind us.

She steps back, putting the illusion of distance between us, her arms wrapping around her stomach. I temper my response, because she's been through hell, and I don't need to add to that.

"Don't let other men touch you," I growl.

Her brows pull together. "I didn't."

"That cunt had his hands on you."

The confusion marring her face surprises me. Did she really not realise what Rug was doing?

"He touched my arm. That's hardly putting his hands on me, Matt."

I close the space between us, my jealousy raging through me, warring with my need to possess her.

I wrap my hand around the side of her neck, tugging her close to me. She doesn't look scared, but she should be. Right now, I feel out of my mind.

"No one fucking touches you, Elyse."

"Why do you care who touches me? We're not together. Let's not read too much into this." I wince. I didn't expect her to throw my own words back at me.

"Everyone knows you walked into this clubhouse with my kid in your belly. That makes you off limits, Elyse." It does. She's my kid's mother. Rug knows better, but I don't understand why I'm so angry either. She's right. We're not together. But as soon as I saw her with that fucker, red filmed my vision and I wanted to cause damage.

She reaches out and wipes her thumb over my lip. "You're bleeding."

I couldn't give a fuck about a little blood. I'm hoping Rug'll be pissing blood for a fucking month.

Cunt.

"This ain't a game, Elyse." I snatch her wrist, stopping her probing of my face.

"I'm not trying to play one," she says, trying to pull free. I don't let her.

"You trying to pit me against my brothers, is that it?"

Her face contorts into anger. "He spoke to me, and I answered. It's called being polite. Something you incidentally know nothing about." She tugs again, and this time, I release my grip on her. "I like your friends. They're nice people."

That's a joke. She was in a room with killers and psychopaths. Nice isn't a word I'd use to describe a single brother in this club.

"Don't let others touch you," I growl.

"Okay, lesson learnt. I won't let anyone near me. I didn't realise that was part of the rules."

She drops her hand to her stomach, and my eyes follow.

"You're carrying my baby, Elyse." I lean my forehead against hers, needing to feel her, needing to be close. My hand still remains on her neck, and she hasn't tried to move me.

"I'm aware of that fact, but I don't know what you

want from me. You hate me one moment, then you're growling at someone for touching my arm. Help me understand."

I pull her closer. "It's easy. I'm the only person who gets to be in your cunt."

Her cheeks heat at my words, and she tries to pull back from my hold, but I don't let her. "Don't be foul."

"Ain't being foul. I'm telling you how it is. Baby or not, my response would be the fucking same."

I watch her eyes as they search my face. "You're giving me whiplash," she admits.

I'm giving myself whiplash.

"Maybe this'll clear shit up."

I smash my mouth against hers. As soon as my lips touch hers, I feel relief flood my body.

She's the drug I crave right now. She's what I need.

She stiffens beneath my forceful kiss for a moment before softening as I thread my fingers through her hair at her nape. Fuck, she tastes exactly as I remember. Maybe a little sweeter. I slide my tongue into her mouth, finding hers. Elyse isn't shy about pressing against mine. She isn't shy about skimming her hands up my back either. She wants me as much as I want her, and that's a fucking good feeling.

I lift her off her feet, easily taking her weight. Her legs wrap around my waist, crossing behind my back, locking her in place. She must be able to feel my growing hard-on against her, because every swipe of her tongue has me becoming solid in my jeans.

Slowly, I walk us over to the bed and lay her on the

mattress like she's precious fucking cargo. I skim my hand over her stomach, pausing as I do for a second. I haven't really considered what it will mean to be a father, but I want it. I know that much.

I want to be a better parent than my own.

I also want to be inside her.

I want to taste that sweet little pussy again. We're heading for a crossroads, one that will determine our future, because once I have her, I'm not going to want to let her go. Is this the right thing?

I peer down at her, loving the soft look on her bruised face. She's still fucking beautiful, even marked as she is. I trail my fingers over her cheeks, mapping every hurt that cunt delivered on her. I'm going to repay that tenfold.

Dipping down, I press my mouth to hers again and devour her like a starving man. The line is crossed. It's too late to go back now.

I lift off her so I can pull her pants down. Her underwear follows a moment later, and I'm staring at her pretty pink cunt.

Fuck.

I bury my face in it, smelling her scent. She's wet, soaked, in fact.

I lick through her folds, tasting her and relishing her juices as they coat my tongue.

Her back arches off the bed as she releases a garbled moan I can't decipher. I part her folds and lick her from front to back, dipping my tongue inside her channel. Then I move to her clit. I circle that little bud over and over, until she's writhing on the bed.

I love her like this. Spread out for me.

I want to be inside her, but I don't want to rush this. I want to take my time with her, and I don't want it to be over too soon.

"Matt..." she gasps. "That's it. Just there."

I increase my pace, my tongue aching as I bring her to climax.

I fucking love eating a woman out, and with Elyse, it's different. I feel connected to her.

As her orgasm starts to fade, I unzip my jeans and shove them down my legs. I've never gone bare before. I've always wrapped, so it feels completely different to enter her without a condom.

Her channel contracts around me as I slide through her wetness, into her cunt. She feels like a silk glove. I shove inside her, my pelvis pressed to her pussy as I bury myself to the root.

"Move," she begs. "Please."

I oblige, dragging my cock out of her, nearly to the tip, before pushing back inside her.

I set a slow pace to start, before increasing to a ruthless rhythm. Each thrust moves her up the mattress, and I have to hook my arms around her thighs to keep her in place. I haven't even undressed her top half or mine. I'm standing with my jeans around my knees as I fuck her hard and fast.

Her moans are a fucking symphony I want to play on repeat, but what surprises me is how she holds my gaze. Her eyes never leave mine, other than to close momentarily or roll in her head. The connection between us is undeniable. I love it.

I've never had sex like it. Not even the first time with her.

I press a hand against her stomach, imagining her swollen belly as our kid grows, and as she comes again, I spill inside her. I realise in this moment that even if she wants to walk away, I'm not going to let her.

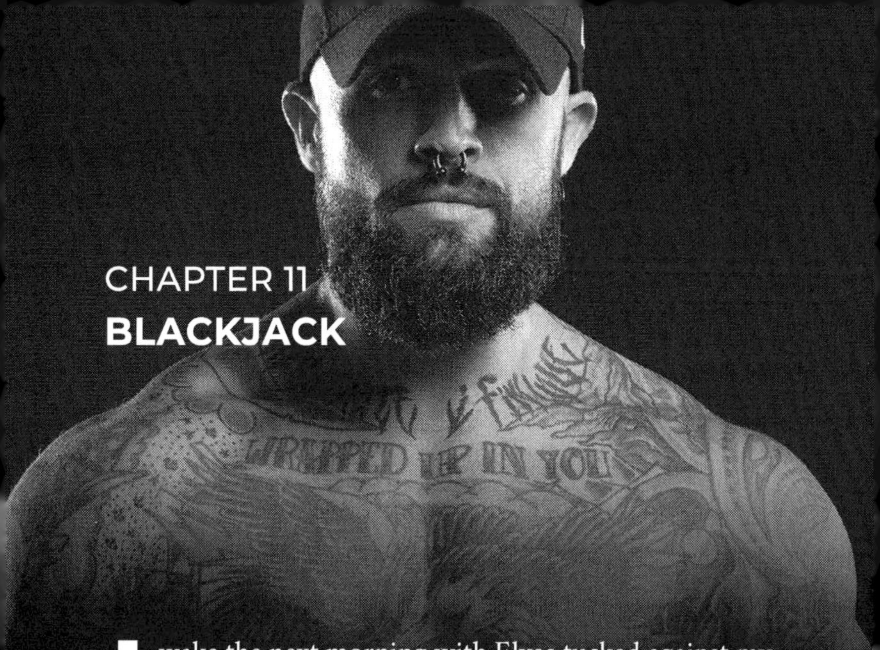

CHAPTER 11
BLACKJACK

I wake the next morning with Elyse tucked against my side. It shouldn't feel as good as it does, but this time I'm the one who is going to steal from the bed.

Carefully, I shift from under her, and once I'm free, I slip out of the bed. I glance at her. She's still asleep, her eyes rimmed with dark smudges that seem less pronounced than they were last night.

I can't resist leaning over and kissing her bare shoulder. It's exposed above the blankets, tantalising. I wish I had time to fuck her again, but I want to get this shit over with and get back to her.

Forcing myself away from her, I dress, pulling my underwear, jeans and tee on before shrugging into my kutte. She doesn't stir the entire time, which I'm grateful for. I want to leave her sleeping as long as possible.

I go to the sofa so I can pull my boots on. I have to admit, I'm worried about her. She looks like hell.

Is it the pregnancy or concern about Howard?

As I lace my boots up, my gaze shifts between her and what I'm doing. I've never had to protect someone before. This is new ground for me, but I want to keep her safe.

Her, my kid, and Aaron.

Standing, I grab my keys and wallet off the side where I left them before we laid together after I fucked her, and slip both into my jeans pocket, before straightening my kutte.

I don't care what it takes. Nothing is going to touch her again.

This Howard fucker is going to regret laying a hand on her.

I slip out of the room, careful as I shut the door behind me. As I step into the common room, streamers and balloons are scattered everywhere. Beer bottles and glasses too. The two prospects are cleaning up, bin bags in their hands as they move around the room, clearing each table as they go.

Amongst all the chaos, I find Howler sitting at the bar. He has a mug of coffee in front of him.

He glances up as I sink down next to him. "Mara and Trick took Aaron home with them last night." I already knew that. Trick messaged me late last night before we went to sleep to tell me. "You sort shit out with your woman?"

My woman.

Fuck.

"Ain't claimed her yet," I tell him.

He side-eyes me. "Brother, you claimed her in front of everyone when you dragged her from the room after Rug spoke to her. You might as well have pissed on her fucking leg." He smirks, which makes me scowl.

That's not why I went postal on him. "Fucker had his hands on her. He's lucky I left him breathing."

"He won't make that mistake again," Howler says. He understands. He would kill anyone if they touched his old lady, and while Elyse isn't officially mine, I don't think there can be any misunderstanding what she is to me.

"The fuck are you doing up so early anyway?" I ask.

"Pia."

I cock a brow. "She kick you out of bed?"

"No, fucker." His mouth pulls into a line. "She's talking to Socket and Valentina."

Things between the three of them are still uneasy, but Pia is trying to rebuild bridges. That's all her parents can demand from her. I know Howler hates leaving her to them, that he'd rather be there to protect her—even from her own blood—but this is something Pia has to do herself, and he knows that.

"They sort shit out?"

"Getting there," he says. "It's going to be a long road. This ain't something they can just whack a plaster over and fix."

"It looks like it was a hell of a party."

"Before or after you dragged Elyse out of here and punched a brother?"

I sigh. "Hitting Rug was fucking shitty of me, but fuck, he's lucky that's all I did. Hope that cunt feels it today."

"You like this one." Howler's observation doesn't surprise me. He's known me a long time.

"She's having my baby."

"Yeah, but you like *her*."

I do, and I'm not going to deny it either. "You done talking about our feelings?"

He shakes his head, laughing a little. "You need to pull your head out of your arse."

"Ain't looking for advice, Prez."

"Too bad. I'm giving it anyway. You meet someone who makes it easier to drag through the muck of this life, you hold onto them. Pia is my fucking world. I'd kill to keep her safe. I'd take a bullet to protect her. If Elyse gives you that same feeling, then you got to hold tight to her, brother. Trust me."

I mull his words over for a moment. I feel all that, and more.

"She's mine," I tell him simply, "and not just because of the kid."

Howler sips his coffee. "Then fucking hold tight."

I plan on it. "I need to find this fuck who is playing with her."

"Give me the details. I'll call around. Someone will know what rock he came out from under."

I tell him everything I know about Howard, which isn't a fucking lot.

"What are you going to do with that fuck when you get hold of him?" he asks when I'm finished.

"Rip his cock off and feed it to him to start with." The words come out on a snarl. I can't help it. I want to kill that fucker for putting his hands on my girl. "He hurt her, tried to rape her. Ain't letting that fucking stand."

Howler's eyes flare with rage. Considering what the Road Jesters did to his woman, I don't blame his anger. "What is it with these fucking degenerate bastards?"

I shake my head. "Fucked if I know." These upcoming wannabe gangsters and clubs don't seem to have any kind of moral code when it comes to women not in the life.

"I'll see what I can find out."

"Thanks, Howler."

I get up from the stool, and when I step back into the corridor, I nearly collide with Terror.

"Fuck, didn't see you there," I say. "But while you're here… want to take a ride with me?"

"Yeah," he says without checking where we're going.

We go out onto the street and make our way to the bikes. I pull my helmet on, securing the chin strap in place before climbing on the back. Terror waits for me to pull out of the space, following behind me.

The ride doesn't take long, the traffic moving freely through the city. The area she lives in is run down, old, cheap.

It belongs to the Masons, a gang who have a small patch of territory on her estate—just a handful of roads. They are allies, which is the only reason they're still here. They fought with us against our enemies.

I feel safe moving through their patch.

I pull up outside the address Elyse gave me when she put together the list of what she needed from the flat. As I glance up at the building, my dismay starts to grow. There's no fucking way she's coming back here.

There are groups of lads hanging around, smoking.

The distinct smell of it tells me it's not cigarettes. Nearly every wall is tagged with art. I glance at Terror, who doesn't let a single emotion slide onto his face as he kicks down his stand and gets off his motorcycle.

"Those bikes better be here when we get back," I say to the lads.

Then Terror and I make our way inside. There's a drunk man passed out in the entranceway, next to the mailboxes. I'm starting to see red. How the fuck is she living here? She shouldn't have to.

I traipse up the stairs, stepping over a broken step before we reach her floor. Terror still hasn't asked what we're doing here, but I can see he's ready for whatever might be about to happen.

As we approach Elyse's flat, nothing looks out of the ordinary. The door is locked tight, and I have to use the key she gave me to gain access to the property.

When I open the door, I realise how much of a cunt this Howard fucker is. The place is trashed. The sofa is slashed up, the bedding on it cut to shreds—was Elyse sleeping on there? There are broken dishes littering the floor and what looks like red wine staining the carpets. I step over the debris, my mouth pulling into a line and my head starting to fire up.

I move into the bedroom—there's only one, which confirms someone was sleeping on the sofa, and judging by the shit in the room, it's not Aaron. His stuff is ruined too. Every scrap of clothing in the chest of drawers has been damaged or defaced in some way.

"Fuck," I mutter.

I'm going to enjoy torturing Howard. I'm going to make it hurt.

I step back out into the living area, which is tiny, barely big enough for the sofa, an armchair and the kitchen behind it.

"This feels personal," Terror notes.

Because it is. He didn't expect Elyse and Aaron to fight back. This fucker thought he'd have easy access to her whenever he wanted it.

"There's nothing to salvage here," I mutter.

"This your girl's place?"

My girl.

Already everyone sees her as mine. That assures me that she'll be taken care of no matter what happens to me.

"Yeah."

"We going to kick the shit out of whoever did it?"

"Yeah," I repeat.

I spot a broken frame on the floor and duck down to my haunches. It's a picture of Elyse, but she's younger—maybe sixteen or seventeen—and she's with a younger kid, who I'm guessing is Aaron.

I pull it free of the glass and debris, tucking it into my pocket.

"Let's go," I say.

Terror follows me to the door. I lock it behind us, and together, we head back to our bikes. The lads are still where we left them, our bikes too.

I pause before getting on mine. "That fucker is pissed."

"Yeah," Terror says. "I'd say so." He grins. "You want me to torture him?"

I snort. "You're too fucking kind."

"It's been a minute. You know I get twitchy if I don't spill blood."

He does. It's not a lie. Terror is exactly what his name suggests. I've seen him use some medieval level shit when it comes to torturing his victims. He's scared the fuck out of me and Howler in the past.

He gets results though.

He replaced Crow, our former sergeant-at-arms. He was jumped at a cash machine, of all things. We were at the tail end of our war for territory. Some jumped up little prick thought he was sending a message. We sent a worse one back. Terror tortured him for days, bleeding him without killing him. Howler and I made him SAA after Crow's funeral.

"What do you want to do?" he asks.

"Until I know where Howard is, there's nothing I can do." The frustration of that pisses me off.

We ride back to the clubhouse, and by the time we reach it, I'm starting to feel more irate. I want this fucker found, and I want to make him pay for what he's done.

I park my bike in the usual spot next to Howler's ride and then head inside with a thanks to Terror. I pause before the door. I don't want to tell Elyse what that cunt did, but she needs to know.

I don't do fucking secrets.

Twisting the knob, I push inside. She's still in bed, but her eyes are open. She smiles as I close the door behind me.

"Hey."

"Hey," I reply, going to the bed. I sink onto the edge of the mattress, and she sits up slightly. She's pulled my hoodie back on, though it's slipped off her shoulder. I want to kiss her there, but I need to talk to her first. "Howard trashed your flat."

"What?"

"The whole place was turned over, all your shit destroyed. I'm sorry."

Her hand goes to her mouth. She kicks the covers off and rushes into the bathroom. I follow her, reaching her as she drops to her knees and retches into the toilet bowl.

I pull her hair back from her face, holding it in my fist, and rub her back with my other hand as she throws up. Fuck, I didn't want to bring this on.

She carries on heaving, but nothing seems to come up. I don't move from her side. When she's done, I flush the toilet and let go of her to grab a towel from the rack. Running the taps, I dip the towel in the water before I sweep her hair off her neck and press it to her nape.

"I'm sorry," she murmurs.

"No need to say sorry. You okay now?"

"Yeah."

"Morning sickness?"

"I guess so. I'd feel better if I could throw up, but it won't come." She turns to face me, leaning against the wall behind her. I pull the towel away from her neck, dropping it in the sink. "Sorry you had to witness my Exorcist impression."

"I don't give a fuck about watching you puke, babe." I

really don't. I've seen brothers do worse over the years. "Do you think you can get up?"

She nods, so I take her hands and pull her up off the floor. She collides with my chest, and I don't let her move back from me. "I'm going to take care of everything," I promise her, tucking her hair behind her ear as I let my eyes crawl over her face.

Elyse peers up at me. "You can't promise that."

I can, because it's going to fucking happen.

She presses her face against my chest, and my arms automatically come around her, drawing her to me.

"I'm so sorry about all of this."

"Ain't none of it your fault."

"It is, Matt. I brought this shit to your door. You shouldn't have to deal with it."

I cup her face. "Baby, your shit is my shit." And there's nothing she can say to change that. "Brush your teeth and I'll take you and Aaron for breakfast."

After that, I'll ring her landlord, get her out of the lease —even if I have to throw down some threats—and send a couple of prospects over to clean out the place. I don't want her fucking worrying about anything.

She smiles and turns back to the basin. I watch as she grabs a new toothbrush from under the cabinet and starts to clean her mouth. I can't keep my eyes off her. I can't stop from moving up behind her, my hands going to her waist.

"Fuck, you're beautiful," I tell her.

I kiss over her bruised cheek, and she stops brushing. "Matt."

"I want to fuck you," I tell her.

Her eyes go heated in the mirror. "So fuck me then."

"Rinse," I order.

She spits the toothpaste out and rinses her mouth. I turn her to face me, her minty breath mingling with mine. "I'm going to have you screaming," I warn her.

"Don't promise me a good time," she fires back. I love these little feisty moments she displays.

I lift her into my arms and carry her into the bedroom, where I fuck her until she's crying my name.

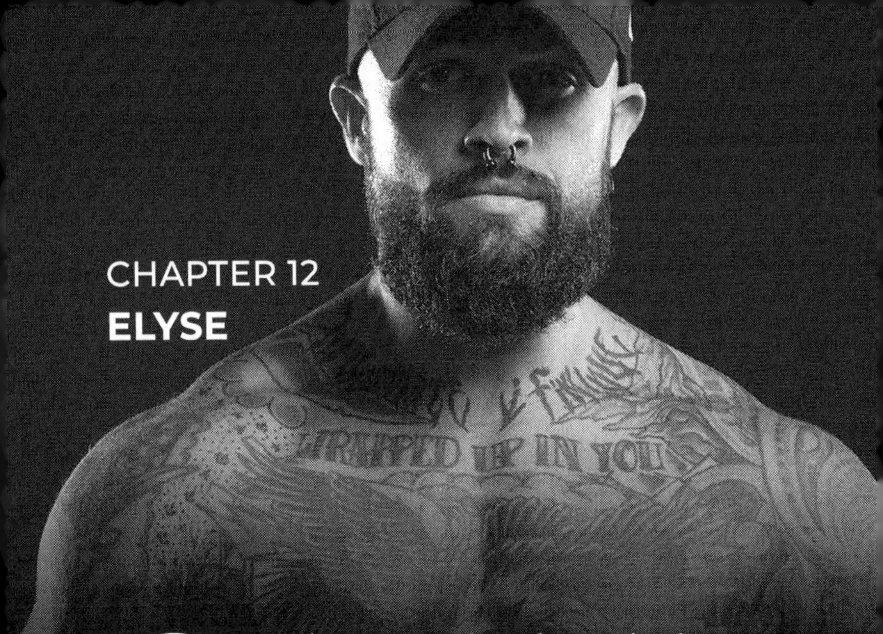

CHAPTER 12
ELYSE

Once I'm clean and ready, we head out to breakfast. Matt has to borrow a car from another brother. As I climb in the passenger side, he gets into the driver's seat.

"I'll sort out getting a car," he says. "The bike ain't family friendly for when we're all together. You're going to need wheels too. Ain't letting you walk around the city with a newborn."

"You don't have to change everything about your life, Matt."

"Unless you want the kid riding the handlebars, we're going to need a car."

"Oh. Good point." I stare at his side profile as he drives through the city. Aaron stayed at Mara's house last night, so we're picking him up before heading to breakfast.

We pull up outside a large semi-detached house in a quiet street. It's one of those old nineteen-thirty style properties with a large bay window on the front and an attached garage. Matt cuts the engine.

"Before we go inside, I need to give you something. I got you a new phone." He reaches over into the back seat and hands me a brand new device. I don't know much about technology, but I can tell this handset is expensive.

"This is too much."

"That fucker knows your number. Don't like him having it or being able to contact you. So far, he's been quiet, but that ain't going to stay that way. He's going to be seething at what Aaron did to him. That anger'll fester until it overflows."

A chill runs through me. I didn't even consider that he might contact me or try to hurt me either. I've been living in a bubble, feeling safe because of Matt, but Howard is still out there and a threat.

"Thank you." I open the box and take the new phone out. Matt shows me how to turn it on.

"I got one for Aaron too," he adds.

An ugly feeling slithers through me. "Matt."

"Don't look at me like that. Ain't poor, babe. I can afford two new fucking phones to keep you and Aaron safe."

I nibble my bottom lip. "I need to sort out work then," I say.

He eyes me. "You want to keep your job, then keep it, but you don't need to work. I got more than enough to support us."

"Matt, I can't just sponge off you."

"Ain't sponging, and I got more than enough to

support us all for the rest of our lives. You want to work then work, but don't do it because you want to pay your way. I won't take any money off you, Elyse. Ever."

"I've got some time off from the office, but Frank won't keep me on at the bar. He's already pissed at me for collapsing on him."

Matt grits his teeth. "You want me to kill this Frank fucker, keep talking."

I sigh. "I don't want you to kill anyone."

Except maybe Howard.

I feel awful thinking that, but I hate him to my core.

"Babe, work, don't work. I don't give a shit. It's up to you, but work because you want to, not because you feel you have to. Come on." He gets out, and I follow him.

He waits for me on the pavement, and we walk together to the door. Mara answers it before we have chance to knock.

"Hey," she says, and then turns and yells, "Kid, your sister's here."

"He been okay?" I ask. I feel a little guilty for just abandoning him last night, but I needed to be with Matt. I needed to sort things out with him.

"Yeah, Aaron is an amazing lad."

As she says that, he appears in the doorway behind her. He's wearing a hoodie that looks too big on him, making me wonder if it's Trick's or Mara's. The hood is up, his hair dripping into his eyes.

"Take care, kiddo."

"Thanks, Mara," he says and slips out of the door.

"Thank you," I say too.

"That's what family is for, and you two are family."

Her words warm me, and I know they will affect Aaron. All he's ever wanted is to belong. To be loved.

"Tell Trick I'll see him later," Matt says.

The three of us walk back to the car. Once we're all inside, I twist to look at my brother in the backseat. "I'm sorry I left you last night."

He waves this off. "Trick and Mara are lit. Trick says he's going to teach me to shoot an air rifle."

I raise a brow and glance at Matt, who shrugs. "Get used to this shit, babe. I got a lot of family and they're all going to want to take care of you."

That's a foreign concept to me. My entire life, no one has ever taken care of me. My parents were as useless as each other. I was living on my own from sixteen. I don't know how to even accept help because I'm so used to doing everything myself.

I turn to look out of the window, not wanting my brother or Matt to see the tears in my eyes. I hate how emotional I am at the moment. I know it's the pregnancy, but I don't want to constantly be crying on everyone.

"You enjoy the party?" Matt asks Aaron.

"Yeah. It was so good." Aaron continues to ramble on about his evening, listing every brother in the clubhouse he spoke to and what he liked about them.

Matt's hand presses against my thigh as my brother talks. I peer over at him, but his eyes are on the road.

My attention goes back to the side window as my hand rests on top of his.

Matt drives us to a small diner type cafe not far from

where Mara and Trick live. He parks in the car park, cutting the engine and pulling up the handbrake. Aaron gets out, and as I go to open the door, Matt stops me.

"No more tears," he tells me.

"I'm sorry."

"No more apologies either." He leans over and kisses me. "Come on, let's get you both fed."

We get out of the car and head into the diner.

Aaron picks a booth near to the door, sliding onto the bench. I sit opposite, Matt next to me. The waitress brings over the menu, and as I look at the prices, I get a hollow feeling in my gut. I don't have enough to cover this.

"I'll have a tea," I say.

Aaron's face drops, and I hate doing it to him, but he knows the drill. We've been in this situation before. "I'm good."

Matt stares between us. "You ain't good. Pick something to eat." He turns to me. "You too."

"Matt... we can't. We don't have the money—"

"Did I ask you for any?" he interrupts.

"No, but—"

"Ain't ever going to ask you to pay for shit, Elyse. You're on my arm, in my bed, you're my responsibility. I pay. You eat. Both of you. Pick something."

The tone of his voice tells me not to argue, but I do anyway. "I don't need a sugar daddy," I say quietly.

He puts the menu down and gives me his attention. "You think that's what this is about?"

I frown. "No." I'm not sure why I even said it.

"Know you're not good at accepting help, but order food or I'll order something for you."

Aaron meets my gaze and wiggles his brows, a smirk on his face.

"You already bought us phones. I'm not a leech."

"No, you're the mother of my child."

"I don't want to just be that either," I say.

Matt glances up at Aaron. "Give us a min, kid."

He surprises me by getting up without argument and moving over to the counter to look at the cakes through the display cabinet.

Matt twists his body so he's facing me. "I fucked you. Last night."

My cheeks heat as I glance around. I don' think anyone heard. "I know that."

"I came inside you."

"Matt." My voice has a bite of warning. Sometimes he's so crass it makes my ears heat.

"Know it hasn't sunk in yet, but I'm all in this, babe. You, me, Aaron and our kid. This is the family I'm trying to build."

My heart warms at his words. "Because your hand was forced."

"Yeah, in a way it was. Would it change my decision? Not even a little. We could have raised this kid apart. Plenty of people co-parent without fucking, babe. If you're in my bed, it's because I want you there."

He kisses me, and I melt against him, unable to stop myself. Every time our mouths fuse together it's like my body forgets sense and rationality. He makes me forget how we met, makes me forget my doubts that he's only with me because of the baby.

He pulls free of me, his forehead resting against mine.

"I don't want you to resent me," I admit.

"Why the fuck would I resent you?"

"A baby is going to change our lives. Turn them upside down. You didn't plan for this."

"No, but we'll figure it out. I want to be a father to this baby."

"If that changes, you don't have to stick around," I say, giving him an out.

"You need to stop talking before I lose my temper," he says, kissing me again. "Pick something to eat too. The waitress will be back in a second."

Matt gestures to Aaron he can come back. My brother slips back into the booth and reclaims the menu.

When the waitress comes back over, Matt orders a full English breakfast. Aaron has pancakes, and I order an egg and sausage English breakfast muffin and a side of fruit—even though the former cancels out the latter.

Throughout breakfast, Matt questions Aaron, finding out more about his life. The conversation between the two of them is easy. I didn't expect that, but I should have. They are similar personalities.

My brother and—I don't know what to call Matt. My boyfriend?—talk all the way through breakfast. We leave the diner and head back to the car.

Matt drives back towards the city centre. Eventually, he pulls the car into an underground parking garage that he opens using a keycode at the gate. He drives into the garage, the headlights flashing on at the change of lighting.

He parks in space 4C and cuts the engine. We pile out of the car, and Matt holds his hand out to me, which I take.

We take the lift up to the third floor and step out into a corridor. This building is nothing like our old one. It's clean, fresh, and modern. He stops before 4C and puts his key into the lock, pushing into the flat.

My eyes are everywhere as we move into the spacious hallway. There's a pile of motorcycle boots and a pair of running shoes near the door. Coats and jackets hang on a rack opposite the front door. It's light, airy. There are doors off the corridor.

Matt steps up behind me, his hands going to my shoulders. "There's two spare bedrooms. Aaron, you can have the bigger of the two for now."

"For now?" I ask.

"Babe, was serious about needing to move. Somewhere out by Trick and Mara would be good."

I think back to their house. It was gorgeous, and it looked spacious from the outside.

I want to argue with him, but Matt is going to do this no matter what I say. In truth, I'm not keen to go back to our old place either. Not when Howard has access to us there. I feel so much relief that we're safe, that someone is going to take care of us, that I start to cry.

"Uh… Elyse? You okay?" Aaron sounds a little freaked.

I try to explain it's pregnancy hormones, but it's not.

This is pure human relief. I'm crying too hard to get the words out anyway.

Matt pulls me against his chest. "What did I say about tears?"

"I'm sorry," I manage to say between sobs. "I'm just… I've been so scared for so long. I finally feel safe."

He kisses my forehead. "Nothing will touch you again. I promise you." It's a promise I know he will keep. He wipes at my cheeks. "Come and see your home."

He gives us a tour. The flat is amazing. The master bedroom is huge, with a king-size bed and a walk-in closet that is bigger than Aaron's old bedroom. There's an en-suite shower room. The two other bedrooms are decent sized. One has a double bed in, the other looks like it's used for storage, though there's a desk pushed against one wall.

There's also a large living area with an L-shaped sofa that can comfortably seat us all with room to spare. Aaron is impressed by the huge TV screen on the wall. It must be sixty inches at least.

Off the living room is a kitchen and small utility room, as well as a family bathroom with a tub. It's so nice, so different from our place. I've done what I can to make it home for Aaron, but I don't have the money to do anything like this.

He barely had anything.

I barely had anything either.

Aaron disappears into the room that's to become his bedroom, leaving Matt and I in the living room. "He can pick whatever he wants for his room," Matt says.

"He's never had so much space." I fiddle with the hem of my hoodie, feeling suddenly nervous. "I can sleep on the sofa until I can get a bed for the third bedroom." I have no idea if I even still have either of my jobs. Frank was pissed I collapsed at work, and I didn't call in sick today to my office job. "I can pick up some extra shifts. It won't take long."

He snaps his eyes to me. "You're in my bed. With me. And you ain't doing extra shifts. You want something, I'll get it for you."

I want to argue with him, but he steps up to me, cupping my jaw with his hands. "You're mine. I take care of you."

"I need to have my independence, Matt. People generally don't stick around in my life. I can't rely on anyone."

"You can rely on me."

I peer up at him, my heart suddenly starting to race. "I want to believe that. I really do, but—"

He silences me with a kiss. "Even if things turn to shit between us, ain't letting you go back to that fucking flat or that fucking life you're running from. You'll always be taken care of, Elyse. Get used to it."

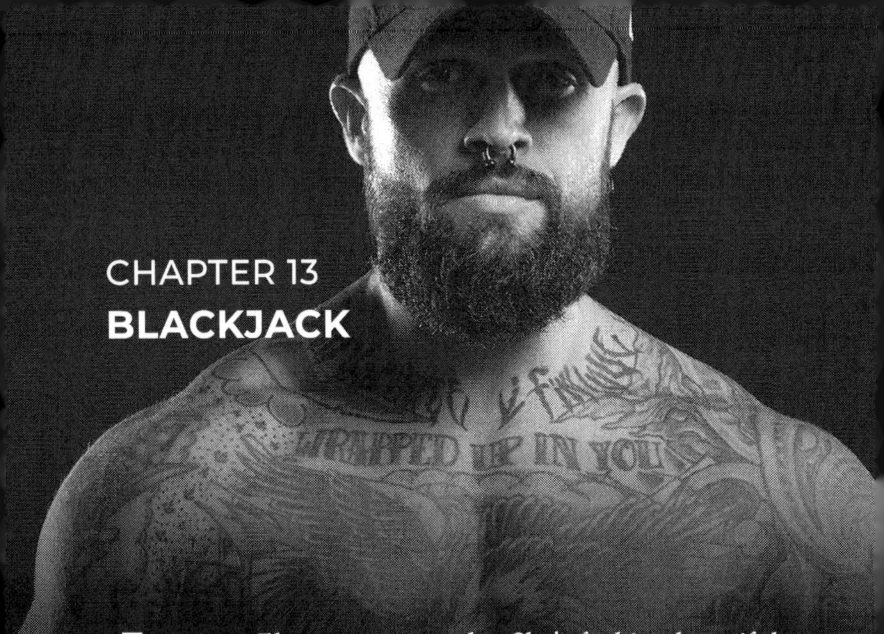

CHAPTER 13
BLACKJACK

I wait as Elyse starts to wake. She's fucking beautiful in the morning—all ruffled and sleepy, like a little door mouse buried in the covers. Her eyes open and blink, before she focuses on me.

She smiles.

"Are you watching me sleep again?"

I've done this every day in the two weeks her and Aaron have been living with me. I can't help it, even if it makes me a creeper.

"You want me to stop?"

She shakes her head. "No."

"Good. I wasn't going to anyway."

She laughs and I pull her on top of me, the blankets falling off her to reveal her body. Her tits have grown over the past few weeks and have become sensitive. I'm careful as I scrape my fingers over her nipple, but she arches her back, pushing herself into my hand.

She's ten weeks pregnant and her belly has started to

grow ever so slightly. If I didn't know every inch of her body, it wouldn't be noticeable, but I can see the small curvature of her stomach, the changes to her body that others might not notice.

I release her tit and press my hand over where our kid is. There's no movement, not yet. Elyse says it won't happen for a while yet, but I can't wait until I can feel our baby moving around inside her.

Fuck, that never gets less strange saying that. It doesn't feel real sometimes. Elyse peers down at me, her eyes heavy and heated.

"It's going to get bigger," she warns.

"Yeah."

"Are you still going to want to fuck me in the mornings when I look like a beach ball?"

I pull her down, so her body is moulded against me. My cock is already semi-solid, waiting for her slick channel to take me.

I poke it against her. "Does this answer your question?"

"What about when I have stretch marks and can't see my feet?" She raises a challenging brow.

"The fuck do you want to see your feet for anyway?" I ask, kissing her face as if she's my oxygen.

She pulls back, stopping me, her hand on my chest. "I'm serious, Matt. I'm not going to be like this for much longer."

Her bottom lip goes between her teeth and my eyes narrow. "You think I'm not going to want you because you're pregnant?"

"I don't know," she admits. "This is new for me."

"For me too, but that shit ain't going to change how much I want to fuck you, babe."

I tug her down so I can kiss her. It's hot, heavy, and she moans against my lips. Her nipples scrape against my chest as she writhes on top of me. I want to eat her pussy, so I roll her onto her back.

She looks beautiful among the pillows. Aphrodite in the fucking flesh. I run my hand over her stomach again, feeling the small curve there. "Babe, I can't wait for you to start showing. I'm already obsessed with this little bump."

Elyse drops a hand over her eyes. "It's probably just bloat. A lot of first-time mum's don't show until between twelve and eighteen weeks."

"You been reading the baby books again?"

"Every day," she says softly. "I want to be prepared for everything that's going to happen."

I don't give a fuck what it is—bloat, the kid, my imagination. I know my kid is in there, growing healthy and strong. I kiss her belly and move down her pubic bone to her pussy. In a few weeks more it will be clear she's pregnant. I'm counting down the days until that happens.

She tenses as I part her folds and dip my tongue into her wetness. I lick around her clit, focusing on swirling around that little nub over and over until she's clinging to the headboard.

She's fucking stunning, laid out like this. Her red hair looks brighter in the morning light, like an angel. My angel.

I take my time eating her out, making sure to pay

attention to the areas that make her twitch and writhe. She's so responsive it's easy to tell what she likes or when I'm close to the right place.

I love eating my girl out. It makes me feel fucking close to her in a way I can't explain. I love having her juices in my beard. I love making her come so hard she sees fucking stars.

It doesn't take her long to go over the edge.

Her legs flop open wide, giving me the best view of her glistening pussy. Fuck, I want to be inside her.

I'm not fully hard yet though. I palm my dick, giving it a tug and twist. Elyse sits up, her hand going over mine. "Let me," she says.

It's the first time she's ever done this to me, and my body readies itself in anticipation. I sit on the edge of the bed as she climbs off and kneels between my legs.

Fuck, she looks so coy, sitting there, naked and on her knees.

She slides her hand over mine and pushes it aside so she's holding my cock. I watch her as she moves up and down my shaft, slightly twisting as she goes. Every movement makes me suck in a breath. My balls feel heavy and tight as she keeps moving her hand over me.

Her eyes move between her task and my face, as if checking I'm okay with this. I am.

I stand, pulling her grasp off me.

"Suck it, babe," I order.

She hesitates for a moment, then slides my dick past her lips. The warm wetness of her mouth makes me groan. Fuck my life…

I can't stop from moving my hips in time with her sucking. I'm careful not to do anything that might make her choke. She ain't a club whore, and she's pregnant.

My hips twitch suddenly, pushing me deeper into her throat. I don't know what the fuck happens next. She stumbles back, scrabbling away from me, her hands covering her face as she sobs.

The fuck?

I go to her instantly, dropping down to my haunches in front of her. I try to pull her hands away. They are now fisted in her hair, as if she wants to tear them out.

"I'm sorry," she gasps through her tears.

She's sobbing hysterically and I have no idea why. Did I hurt her? What the fuck did I do?

"Elyse?"

"I… I just need a minute."

I'll give her all the time she wants, but I'm starting to panic a little. "Did I hurt you?"

She shakes her head, leaning it against her knees. I don't understand what the fuck is going on, but all my instincts tell me to tread carefully. I don't touch her. Her breath tears out of her in rasps that make me wince.

I know what's wrong with her.

I grab the back of her neck and shove her head low between her knees.

"Breathe," I order. "In and out. Slow breaths."

She does as I order, trust shining in her eyes that I don't deserve. It feels like it takes forever for her to calm down. My heart is pounding until she starts to slow her breaths.

"You had panic attacks before?" I ask when she's a little more under control. She shakes her head. "Did I trigger it?"

Tears fill her eyes. "Yes and no."

"Talk to me, Elyse."

She lets out a shaky breath. "I can't."

"Babe. No secrets between us."

I watch as she rakes her fingers through her hair, her eyes closing for a second. "When I couldn't pay, Howard made me…" She breaks off, her words cracking.

"Made you what?"

"Suck…" That's all she gets out before her breathing starts to pick up again. Fuck, is she going into another attack?

"Suck?"

Her eyes drop to my cock, and the realisation hits me like a fucking wrecking ball. He made her suck his cock.

Fuck.

That cunt is dead.

I'm going to cut his balls off and—

"If this changes things between us, I understand," she says in a small voice. "I thought I could keep myself under control, but it brought everything back. The way he…"

She closes her eyes. She looks so delicate, so small as she hugs her knees.

"It changes nothing," I tell her. Other than how I'm going to kill this fucker. "How many times?"

Her eyes pop open. "Does it matter?"

"I need to know how many times I'm going to slice that fuck's cock up."

Elyse swipes at the tears streaming down her face. "I'm so fucked up."

Caution goes out the window. I drag her into my arms and pull her against me. "No, you fucking ain't."

She sobs against my chest as we sit in a heap on the floor of our bedroom. I hate hearing her breaking like this. My own chest feels tight, my blood like it's boiling. I try to keep my anger at bay to comfort her.

Guilt washes through me. I was so shit to her when she came looking for help, and this is what she was going through.

She wasn't scared of not having the money because he'd beat her. She was terrified he'd sexually assault or rape her.

I hold her against me like the precious fucking cargo she is. "He won't get near you again, Elyse," I promise.

"How can you stop him? I still owe the money."

"That debt should never have been yours in the first place."

"No, but Howard has made it mine."

"Babe, you ain't the first person we've pulled out of something similar."

Her eyes snap up to meet mine. "Who?"

"Pia. She was taken as payment for her ex's debt. The club who took her, hurt her too." I don't give her the nasty details of what the Road Jesters did to Pia. That ain't my story to tell. "We burnt their clubhouse to the fucking ground and destroyed every member of that club. We'll do the same to Howard. I have many brothers who will fight at my back. Not just in Manchester, but around the UK—

even in the States and Europe. The Sons ride as one, babe. Howard's coming at an army."

The relief on her face chokes me. "I've been so scared."

"I know, but all you need to worry about now is our baby and your brother. And maybe picking a new house for the four of us."

"The flat's fine."

"For now, yeah, but what about when our kid is two or three and wants to run around the garden we don't have?"

She ducks her head. "You're really thinking ahead."

I lift her chin, forcing her eyes up. "Babe, you are my future." I kiss her. "Go and get showered. I'll order breakfast in."

"But we never finished what we were doing."

Does she think I'm going to fuck her while she's falling apart? I'm not a total shit head.

"Babe, shower."

I help her stand, and she rolls to her toes to kiss me. "I'm sorry."

"Ain't none of this your fault. Not a single part of it."

Her expression tells me she doesn't believe that.

I watch her disappear into the bathroom and wait for the shower to turn on. Then I grab some clean underwear, slipping it on before I snag my phone off the bedside table. I dial Howler.

He answers after a minute.

"Do you have any idea how early it is?" he grouches. I hear Pia next to him, asking if everything's okay.

"I need you to find this Howard fuck faster," I tell him.

"Why?"

"Fuck is a pervert, Howler. He forced my woman to give him head to clear parts of the debt. I want him dead."

There's a beat of silence, then he speaks. "Howard is an alias, Blackjack. It has to be. Ain't found a single thing about some fuck called Howard doing backhanded deals. No one has heard of him. We need to get clever."

"What do you have in mind?"

"We lure him in."

I know what he's suggesting, and the thought makes rage flare through me. "You want to use my pregnant old lady as fucking bait?"

"Didn't say it was a perfect plan."

"No way. I'm not putting her or my kid in danger, Howler."

"She won't be in danger. We'll make sure of it."

"How?"

"Leave the details to me. I promise nothing will happen to her, but the quickest way to flush him out is through her. She's still in danger while he's running around, brother."

He's right about that. She's terrified of sending Aaron to school, even though we've moved him to a different one.

"Trust me, Blackjack. We can do this."

Fuck. "I do trust you. There's no one I trust more," I admit.

"We'll save your girl and dispose of this fucker at the same time."

"Yeah. Okay."

"And Blackjack?"

"Yeah?"

"Make shit official with Elyse."

"She's my old lady, Howler. It's already fucking official."

"Put a property patch on her back. It'll make things easier if we need to call in reinforcements if she's yours through the proper channels. You know it will. I'll call a vote at the table this morning to get things cemented, but call Judy. Get her rag ordered."

He hangs up.

Judy is old lady to Steam. She's a seam mistress and she's who orders our kuttes.

Since I had to replace all of Elyse's wardrobe when she moved in with me—Aaron's too—I know what size she is. So, when I call Judy, I give her the details and she gives me a waiting time of two days.

It feels too long.

The sooner that patch is official, the better.

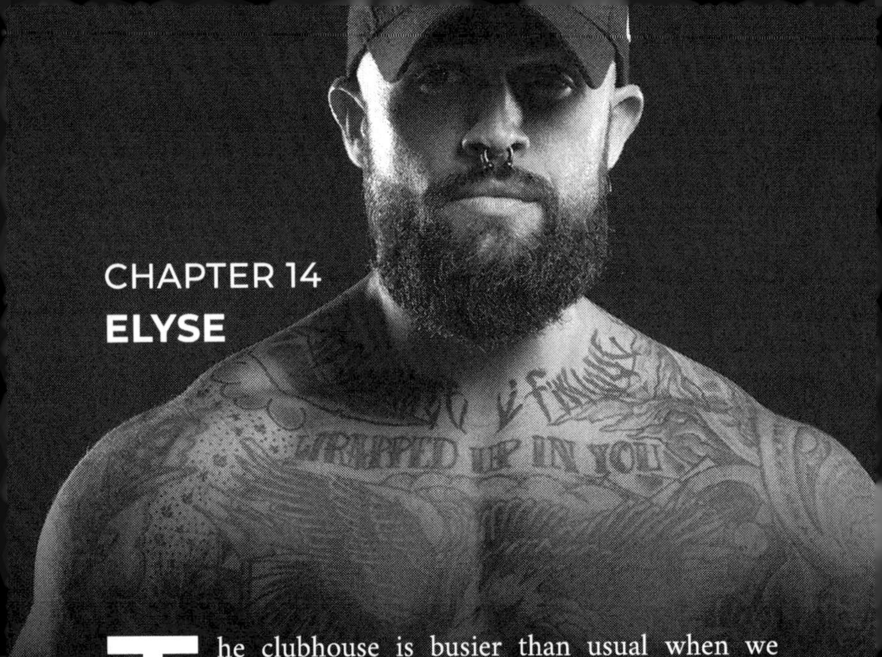

CHAPTER 14
ELYSE

The clubhouse is busier than usual when we head down the next day. There are usually brothers milling around and a few club bunnies, but it seems busier today, and I can't see a single bunny either. Instead, there are old ladies and families.

Aaron is chattering endlessly about some new game he's obsessed with, but I zone him out as Matt and I cross the room hand-in-hand. Howler is sitting at the bar with Pia, Terror and Brewer. Everyone turns to face me.

"Give me a second with her," Pia says, which confuses me. Pia and I are becoming friends, so it's not unusual that she wants to talk to me. It's the edge to her voice that is.

Howler nods and Matt raises my hand to his mouth, pressing a kiss to my knuckles before letting me go.

Pia takes my free hand and pulls me out of the room and into the corridor. Once the doors are shut behind us, she speaks. "Try not to freak out, but Blackjack is about to give you his property patch."

I blink. "What does that mean?"

"It means he's officially claiming you in front of the club. In the eyes of the Sons, it means you're like his wife. Even if he never puts a ring on your finger and legally marries you, you'll still be seen as that in club eyes."

"Matt wants us to be married?"

"This is bigger than marriage, Elyse. You'll become part of the club, under the club's protection. Not just in Manchester but all their other chapters too. It's the only way to keep you and your baby safe."

To keep me safe, he's marrying me in club eyes… not because he wants me.

Because of our child.

How could he want me? We've only known each other a short time. I lied to him. I made him think I wanted him just to steal from him. I've been nothing but trouble since I crashed into his life. I'm dirt, covered in filth because of Howard.

Doubts assail me, and I sink back against the wall.

Pia grabs for me as I slide down to my bottom, bringing my knees up.

"Why is he doing this?"

The confusion that mars her face is unmistakable.

"To protect you."

I peer up at her through wet lashes. "If there was no baby, he wouldn't need to do this."

Pia crouches in front of me. "I don't think that's remotely true."

"Is he only doing this to keep his child safe?"

Her eyes flare. "Honey, no. This isn't something he can dip out of if he changes his mind. It has to go to a club vote. There are very real repercussions of making someone an old lady officially. It's a serious deal. These men don't just put a property patch on anyone. There are women in this club who have been dating their men for years but don't have them."

"Property patches?" I wrinkle my nose. That sounds so archaic.

She nods. "He'll give you a kutte with his property patch on. I didn't want you to see it and get pissed off, but I didn't realise you were doubting him."

"I don't know what I'm feeling. My brain is all screwy. I want to believe he's with me because of me."

"Has he given you any reason to think that's not the case?"

I think back to how he's been over the past few weeks with me. "Well, no. I just… we didn't get off to the best start and now he's doing everything for me. I feel useless. Like a user even."

She huffs out a breath. "I understand that, but these men like to take care of their women, Elyse. I don't pay for anything either. Nor does Mara, even though she works and has her own money. Jake would murder me for even suggesting I pay for things. They're proud men. Old fashioned in a lot of ways, but it doesn't make you a user."

"Why would he do this?" I ask.

Her face softens. "Because he loves you."

My body jolts. "What?"

"He loves you. Anyone with eyes can see it."

I mull that over for a second. He loves me?

Does he?

No one has ever loved me. Not my parents. Not a man. Aaron maybe, but he's my brother.

"I love him too," I admit for the first time. "Old lady, wife, property—I don't care what label we put on it. I just love him. I didn't think he felt the same."

The door opens and Matt steps through. His eyes harden as soon as he sees me on the floor. "What's wrong?" he demands, crouching in front of me.

"I'll give you both a moment to talk," Pia says. She squeezes my hand before she straightens and heads back into the room.

Matt's eyes stay locked on me.

"Elyse?"

"Are you just with me because of the baby?" I ask. My voice wobbles with fear as I ask the question that scares me most.

He blows out a breath. "No."

"If there was no baby, would we be together?"

I bite my bottom lip as I wait for his reply, terrified of what he might say. "Where's this coming from?"

"Pia told me about the property patch. I don't want you to give it to me just because I'm pregnant, Matt."

"I'm not."

"Then why?"

"Babe, the moment I saw you in that casino you turned my fucking cock solid. I wanted you there and then."

"Lust doesn't mean you have to make me your old lady."

"Ain't lust I feel for you. Yeah, our circumstances were unusual. Yeah, the baby has sped shit up, but waking up with you every morning makes me feel like the luckiest bastard on the fucking planet, Elyse. Not because of the baby, but because of you."

He cups my face, and I can't help from leaning into his touch. "I'm sorry. I don't know where my head is at lately."

"You're going through a lot. Cut yourself some slack," he says.

"I don't want you to feel like I've trapped you."

"Fuck… I don't feel like that, babe. If I didn't want to be with you, I wouldn't be. We could easily raise a baby without being together. Parents do it across the world. I'm with you because I want to be. Because I'm starting to fall in love with you," he admits.

My stomach fills with butterflies, each one beating frantic wings against my stomach. "You're falling in love with me?"

He reaches out and plays with a strand of my hair. "Yeah, I am. I feel so fucking protective over you, Elyse. I would kill anyone who tried to hurt you. Never felt that way about anyone. Never understood I could feel like that until now. I see a future with us, our baby, and your brother. A family."

Tears prick my eyes. I want that so badly, but I don't want to hope it could happen.

"I didn't move you into my flat because of the baby. I

could have put you up in a flat somewhere else. I want you living with me, in my bed, waking up with me."

"I want that too," I assure him.

He leans his forehead against mine, his hand cupping my face still. "I think we can have something good between us, babe. We already do. These past few weeks, since you moved in, have been everything I wanted."

"I've never had a family, Matt. Other than Aaron, my whole family suck. I've never had anyone love me. I'm scared of falling for you and you leaving."

He kisses me, and he must be able to taste the salt from the tears streaming down my face. "I'm not going anywhere, babe. I promise. I want my patch on your back to show the world you're mine, to show my club family, who has my fucking heart and soul."

My stomach flutters again. "You're going to make me cry more."

"No more tears," he orders. "I know shit's moving fast, but I'm not unsure about anything between us. This is exactly where I want to be. I wouldn't put my patch on you if I didn't want it too. The club will protect you no matter what, because they support me, but this makes shit more official. If another brother touches you once I've claimed you, there are repercussions. It holds weight, too, with our other chapters. Be my old lady?"

I lick my lips, my mouth suddenly feeling dry. "Yes."

He grins. "Come on, get off the floor."

He helps me up, and then he pins me against the wall behind me, grinding his cock against my pussy. I moan. I can't stop it from coming out of my mouth. "You're mine, Elyse. Don't ever forget it."

He shoves his hands down the front of my leggings and into my underwear. His fingers stroke through my folds, making me gasp.

"Anyone could come out," I say as he strokes me. I grab his wrist, but I'm not sure if it's to make him do more to me or stop what he's doing.

"I don't give a fuck."

"Matt…"

"This cunt belongs to me," he murmurs in my ear, making my blood heat. "Say it."

"Yes." I breathe out the word as he pushes two fingers inside my pussy. Pinned against the wall as I am, I feel surrounded by him. It makes me feel safe. Wanted. Cherished.

"The words, Elyse."

"It belongs to you."

"Good girl."

He pistons his fingers inside me, over and over. The thought there is a room full of people on the other side of the wall heightens my desire. The risk of being caught is dizzying.

I feel my orgasm building fast.

"You belong to me," he adds as he kisses down my neck.

"I love you," I blurt.

He doesn't stop his movement inside me. He just keeps finger-fucking me, pushing so deep inside me I have to widen my stance.

"I love you too, Elyse, and when I get that patch on your back, everyone will know it too."

He brings me to orgasm embarrassingly fast. My body feels alive in ways it never has since I got pregnant. Everything is so much more sensitive, or maybe it's just that Matt is a considerate lover in a way none of my previous boyfriends have been.

Matt slides his fingers out of me and sucks them into his mouth, tasting me. His eyes remain locked to mine. I swallow hard.

"I can't believe you just did that."

"Tasted my girl?"

I lick my lips, and he watches the movement before dipping his head and kissing me. He kisses me until my legs are jelly, until I'm clinging to him like he's the only thing grounding me.

When he pulls back, I'm breathless.

"Come and get my patch, babe."

I nod. "Okay."

He fixes my leggings in place and then takes my hand in his. We step back into the common room, and all eyes come to us. My cheeks heat. I wonder if it's written across my face that he just got me off in the corridor.

"I'm making Elyse my old lady," he says. Cheers go up, glasses raise. He tucks me against his side, his arm holding me tightly in place. "Club voted on it."

He lets me go as Howler steps forward with a thin white box. Matt takes it from him before he turns to me. "Open it."

With trembling fingers, I pull the lid free from the

bottom of the box. There's white tissue paper inside, protecting the garment. I have to peel it back to get to the leather vest. I pull it out and turn it to the back. It's identical to Matt's, but the patches are different. It has the Untamed Sons arced over the top of the insignia, then under, it says, 'Property of Blackjack'.

I glance at him, and his eyes are bright with emotion.

"Put it on," he says.

I hand Howler back the box and turn while Matt helps me into the vest. It fits perfectly, the leather creaking with each movement.

"How do I look?" I ask.

He rubs his thumb over his bottom lip as he takes me in. "Fucking perfect." He kisses me as cheers erupt around the room. "Mine," he says.

I nod. "Yours."

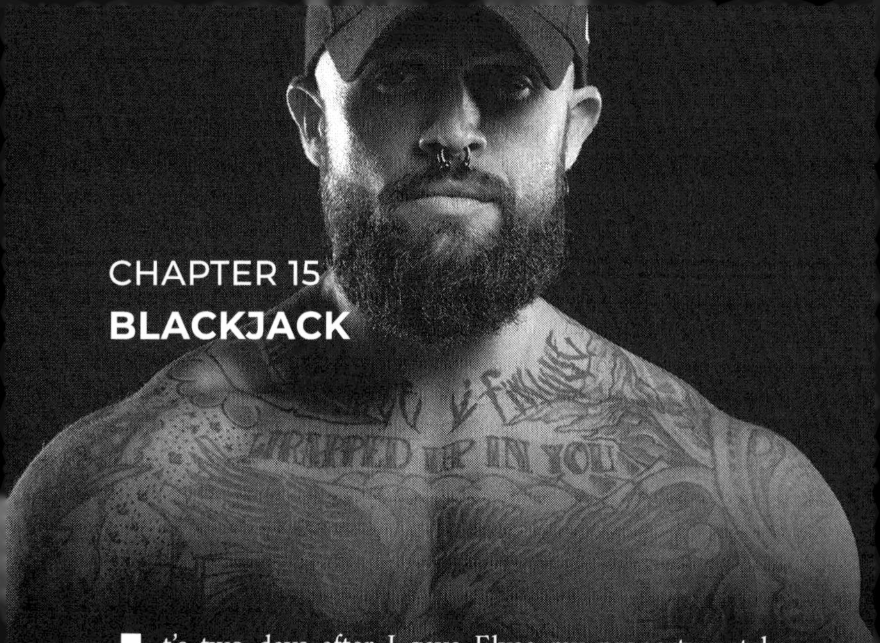

CHAPTER 15
BLACKJACK

It's two days after I gave Elyse my property patch when Howler calls me into his office. I close the door behind me and sink down into the chair in front of his desk.

"I've got things in place to draw Howard out."

"What things?" I demand, sitting up straight in the chair.

"She has his number, right?"

"On her old phone, yeah, but that's been switched off since she came to the club."

"You have it?"

"Yeah, I keep it at the clubhouse."

"We're going to ambush him."

"Where and how?"

"Elyse needs to call him, ask him for money. We'll give her the place to meet. It'll be swarming with our boys."

"He's going to be fucking suspicious if she just reaches out to him for money, Howler."

"She's pregnant. Homeless. Alone—or so she'll tell him. That's going to be a good reason to reach out to a loan shark."

I scrub a hand over my beard.

"Fuck, Howler. I don't fucking like this. I don't want her near him. I promised I'd protect her."

"She won't be anywhere near him. She just needs to make one call. She won't be at the meet. She won't be near it at all."

"I don't even want her talking to that cunt. He abused the fuck out of her, Prez. She's traumatised by that cunt. Ain't putting her back in that nightmare."

"He needs to hear her voice, Blackjack, to set the trap."

I mull this over, my jaw tight. Fuck, I don't like this shit at all. "It'll be over after this?" I ask.

Howler nods. "Yeah."

"Fine. I'll ask her, but she says no then you've got to find another fucking way, you hear?"

"Absolutely, brother."

I push up from the chair and make my way into the common room where I left Elyse sitting with Aaron. She glances up as I come in.

I don't want to take that smile off her face, so I don't tell her the plan. I'll talk to her tonight.

She must be able to sense my unease, though, because she asks, "Everything okay?"

"Perfect," I lie. I glance at Aaron. "You want to learn to ride, kid?"

His eyes flare. "Whoa. Really?"

"Yeah. We've got a couple of spare rides in the garage."

"Is that a good idea?" Elyse asks.

"Ain't going to let him get hurt."

"I know," she says in a soft voice. The trust she has in me, slays me. I can't believe she gives it to me every day freely.

"You have fun with Pia," I tell her. "Don't leave the clubhouse."

She rolls her eyes. "We're just going to sit and talk. She and Howler are looking at houses. I figured I could look too."

The last part is said in a small uncertain voice.

"Something with a big garden, babe," I say, kissing her before I straighten.

I grab Aaron's neck. "Come on, kid."

We head out to the front of the clubhouse. Brew left the bike parked up for me. It's not a spare ride. It's a brand new dirt bike I bought for the kid, but Elyse has an issue with me spending money. I will tell her, but not now. I want her to have a good day with Pia.

"Holy shit!" Aaron exclaims as he spots the bike.

"It's yours, but don't tell your sister."

"Seriously?"

"Yeah, kid. There's a dirt bike track outside of town. You get the hang of riding, and I'll take you on the weekends."

He reaches out, as if to touch it, then pulls his hand back. "Thanks, but I can't."

I frown at him. "Why not?"

"Money and shit comes with conditions."

"Kid, the only condition I have is that you wear a

fucking helmet when you're riding it. I see you without one, the bike's gone."

He looks so torn, then mutters, "Deal."

"You want to go to the track now?" I ask.

He snaps his head around so fast he nearly breaks his neck. "Really?"

"Your sister and Pia will be talking for hours. Might as well do something fun."

Brew helps me load the bike into the back of one of the club's vans, and I drive Aaron to the track.

They get him into all the gear, the protective jump suit, pads for his elbows, shins and knees. Lastly, I hand him the helmet I bought him. If he likes what he does today, I'll get him his own suit and protective shit.

I stand back and watch from the side lines as the kid listens to the instructor. It takes him a few goes to ride without wobbling, but he's a natural.

Watching Aaron makes me think about my own kid and whether I'll be doing shit like this with him or her.

Fuck, I wasn't sure I'd ever be a parent, but the more I get used to the idea, the more I'm excited about the prospect. I'm going to be a hell of a dad to my kid. I'm going to love it with everything I have, be different from my own parents. I can't imagine ever doing a thing to hurt my child. It isn't even born yet and I already love it more than I can put into words.

That's why we need to get Howard out of the picture. So far, I've kept Elyse safe by being with her all the time, but that can't continue. She needs to have a life, one that doesn't include me as her twenty-four/seven bodyguard.

Not that I mind, but Howler's been good with me about cutting back on club duties, but that can't continue forever. I'm VP. I'm needed.

Howard has to die.

Howard and anyone else who might be a threat to her.

I'll burn the whole city to the ground if I have to.

At the end of the session, Aaron walks the bike over to me, his suit spattered with mud. He puts the stand down and leans it over before he flips up the visor on the helmet.

The grin on the kid's face shatters my fucking stone heart into pieces. It makes me angry at his and Elyse's father. Has this kid ever had a good experience in his life?

"Done?" I ask.

"Yeah," he pants. "I can't believe I rode!"

I load the bike into the van while Aaron goes to clean up and get changed. When he wanders back over in his jeans and hoodie, he's still beaming.

"Hey, Matt. I just… I wanted to…" He frowns, and then he surprises the shit out of me by hugging me.

I freeze for a second, before I wrap my arms around him. "You're fine, kid."

"Thanks."

The drive back is noisy. He talks nonstop about everything he did, as if I wasn't watching him. It's nice to see. He's usually kind of quiet, serious. This side of him makes me smile.

I let him out of the van outside the clubhouse front door and watch as he heads inside before I park the van in the garage down the side of the building.

I take a moment before stepping out of the van. I don't want Elyse to worry about anything, but she needs to know what's coming.

I don't want to stress her or the baby, but Howard is a bigger threat right now.

Pulling the keys free of the ignition, I climb out of the van, locking it up, and shut the garage door behind me. I head into the clubhouse and into the common room. Elyse is nowhere to be seen, and my heartrate stutters.

"Relax, she's in the garden," Brew says, coming up behind me. I glance towards the windows that look out over the garden and see she's sitting at a bench with Pia and her brother. Aaron looks like he's talking at her nonstop.

"Fuck," I mutter, scraping a hand over my jaw.

"She's safe here, brother," Brewer tells me.

I turn to him. "I know." Ain't a man in this building who would stand by and let a single thing happen to my woman. "They're my fucking world," I say, meaning every word of it.

"Yeah, you're a lucky bastard. Some people go their whole life and never find that."

I know I'm lucky. If it wasn't for that meeting at the casino, I wouldn't be standing here right now, looking at my girl through the window, thinking about how I want to be inside her pussy.

I always want to be inside her pussy.

I hand Brew the keys to the van, knowing he'll put them back where they belong, and then head out to the garden. I hear Aaron as soon as the door swings back.

Elyse glances up as I approach, and the happiness shining in her eyes nearly fucking knocks me over. She mouths "Thank you" at me. Fuck, she's thanking me for doing something as basic as taking a twelve-year-old kid out to have fun.

I ruffle Aaron's hair as I pass him, taking a seat next to Pia. "Sounds like Aaron and you had fun," Pia says.

"We did! I'm going to learn how to do jumps once I'm good at riding!" Aaron exclaims.

"You did good, kid," I tell him.

"I'm starving," he says. "There any food in the kitchen?"

Pia smiles. "I'm sure I can find something for you. If not, shall we see if I can convince Jake to order some pizza?"

Aaron grins. "I'll be back," he says to his sister, before he and Pia head back inside.

I reach across the table and grab Elyse's hand, needing to touch her, needing to feel her close to me.

"He had a good time," she says. "I never had the ability to do anything like that for him."

"Anything you want to do, just do it, babe. Money ain't an issue."

She lifts our joined hands and kisses my knuckles. It's something I do to her often and it feels amazing to have her do it back.

"You look tense," she says after a moment. "Was Aaron trouble for you?"

I shake my head. "The kid is great."

"Then what's wrong?" She squeezes my hand a little tighter.

"We've found a way to get to Howard," I admit.

She instantly stiffens. "Oh."

"Babe, I don't want to upset you, but we need to go through this shit. It's important."

Elyse glances away, her eyes going over the garden. She doesn't release my hand as she does. "I knew he needed to be dealt with. I just… I got lost in our bubble, I guess."

"I love that I've made you feel safe enough that you have a bubble. And you're going to stay that way. Nothing or no one is getting near you. I promise."

She nods, her trust in me unflappable.

"What do you need me to do?"

"We have to turn your old phone on. We need to call him and arrange a meet."

She swallows hard. "Okay, I can do that. I can meet him."

"Babe, you ain't meeting him. You just need to set one up."

"I'm not?"

"Fuck no. Ain't putting you anywhere near that cunt ever again."

Relief flickers in her eyes. "I'd do it if you need me to, but I'm just as happy not to be near him again. Especially after last time."

I have to breathe through my nose to control the anger bubbling through me. For his attempted rape, I'm going to fuck him up.

For his forced blow jobs...

There isn't enough torture in the world I can give to fix it, but I'm sure as fuck going to try.

"Howler wouldn't put you in a situation where you're going to be in trouble," I say. "I wouldn't allow it anyway. You and my baby are all I fucking care about."

She nods, looking on the verge of tears. "I can do this," she assures me.

I'm not sure about that, but she has to. It's the only way to find this cunt. He's like a wraith. If Howler couldn't find him with all the contacts he has, there's no fucking chance he'll ever be found.

"When do we do this?" she asks, swiping at her tears.

"Now, babe."

She steels her spine. "Okay."

I stand from the bench and wait for her to climb out from the picnic table too. Tucking her against my side, we head back into the common room. Howler is sitting with Pia and Aaron, leaning back in his chair, his arm leaning along the back of Pia's. He meets my gaze as we step back inside, and I nod, telling him without words that it's time. He stands, kissing Pia, and gestures for us to follow him. I lead Elyse into Howler's office, shutting the door behind us.

Howler offers her the seat in front of his desk as he leans against the front of it. "You ready to do this?" he asks.

She nods, licking her lips as if her mouth is dry.

I grab a bottle of water from the mini-fridge behind the desk and hand it to her. She's shaking that much she can't open it, so I take it from her and uncap it before handing it back. She takes a long sip, recaps the bottle, and says, "What do I say?"

He goes through what she needs to tell him over and over until she remembers it word for word. My gut churns. I don't want her fucking talking to that piece of shit.

Howler meets my eyes. "She's ready," he says.

I pull Elyse's old phone from my kutte pocket and turn it on.

It takes an eternity to load, and I wonder how she coped with this piece of shit phone.

After the loading screen appears, the messages start flooding in. Beep after beep. Some are from work, from her dickhead boss Frank telling her she's fired. But most come from Howard.

Bitch, you're dead.

I'm coming for you.

I want my money.

I'm going to slit your throat and rape your corpse.

I own your cunt and I'm coming to collect.

I'm going to kill your brother while you watch.

On and on the messages go. I fucking snarl. I can't help it. I want to kill this fucker even more after reading the filth he's sent her.

"Are they all from Howard?" she asks in a small voice

as the beeps of incoming messages continues.

I clear the notifications and hand her the phone. “Dial him and put it on loudspeaker.”

She takes the phone, her chest heaving as she does. She hits his contact details and dials, before pressing the loudspeaker button.

The ringing fills the room, before the sound of the call connecting.

“You fucking whore,” is Howard’s opening words.

I grit my teeth, my mouth pulling into a snarl as Elyse glances at me.

Dead. He’s dead.

“I should have fucked you bloody.” He hisses the words down the phoneline. It takes everything I have not to jump in.

“I… I need help,” she says, her voice trembling.

Howard laughs. “That’s fucking rich. You left me bleeding on the floor of your fucking flat.”

“I was scared.”

“Girl, you don’t know fear. I’m about to show you just how fucking scared you should be.”

His words seem to unlock something in her, and her spine snaps straight. “Considering you tried to rape me, you’re lucky you’re breathing at all.”

“Isn’t rape. I own your cunt. I own everything about you until your daddy’s debt is repaid.”

Howler circles his finger in the air, telling her to get to the points he gave her. “I’m pregnant,” she says.

“Am I supposed to congratulate you?”

“No, but I need… I need money. I’m homeless. I need

help. Please."

There's a beat of silence, and I wonder if his suspicion is raised. "Fuck, you must be desperate to ask me."

"I can't let my baby die, Howard. I need somewhere safe. You need to cancel my father's debt. It's not mine, and I shouldn't have to pay it."

"You want to cancel your father's debt to pay a whole new one?"

"No. I don't want to pay anything."

"Bitch, do you think I'm fucking stupid?"

"No, but I have a different deal for you." She glances at me, and I nod, telling her to continue. "I'll be yours if you help me."

There's a pause, so long that I think he's hung up. "You won't fight or fucking cry anymore?"

I ball my hands into fists.

"Because honestly, that shit was such a fucking turn off."

Elyse closes her eyes. "I won't fight or cry. I promise. Just help me with my baby, please."

"Okay, you've got a deal."

"I don't have the flat anymore, but I've been staying in an old warehouse outside Ancoats." She gives him the address word perfect. "Meet me tomorrow at eleven."

"Fine. The kid can't come though. Your brother. He's not part of this."

"Howard, he comes, or I don't."

He scoffs down the line. "You really think you have room to negotiate?"

"We're a package deal. No Aaron, no me."

I glance at Howler, but he's watching Elyse intensely.

"Fine, the brat can come, but you keep him out of my way."

"Agreed."

"I'm going to enjoy wrecking your cunt, bitch."

He hangs up.

Elyse sags in her seat, her hand going to her chest. I go to her, scooping her immediately into my arms. "You did great, babe," I tell her.

"I was scared," she admits.

"I know, but he bought it."

"I had to fight for Aaron. He'd know otherwise."

"You did great," I repeat.

"What's next?" she asks, even as she clings to me, her arms wrapped tight around my back.

"For you, nothing. He ain't something you need to worry about," I tell her.

She snuggles against me. "Thank you, both of you."

"Ain't a problem," Howler says. "You're family, Elyse. Sons take care of family."

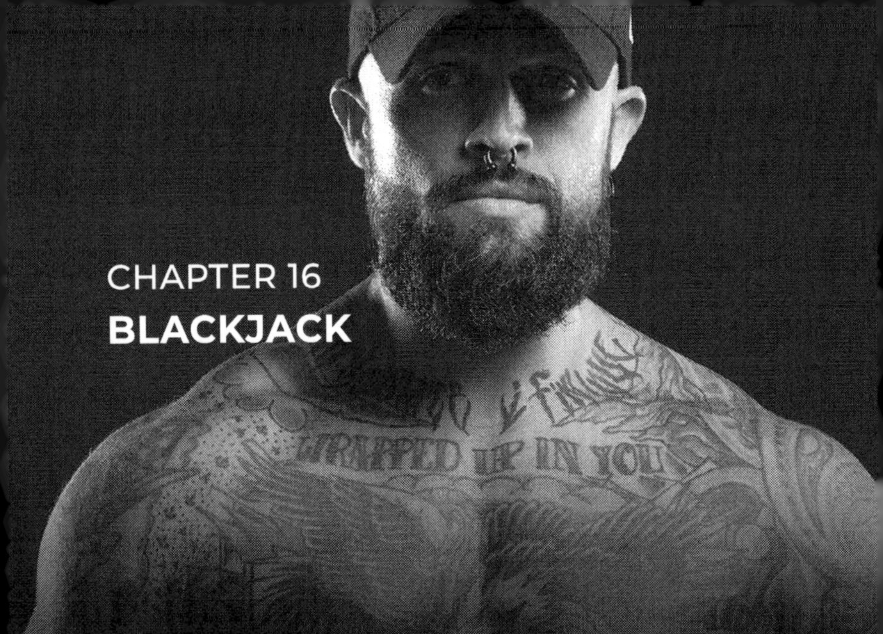

CHAPTER 16
BLACKJACK

I wake the next morning with Elyse pressed against me. She didn't sleep well last night. The call with Howard fucked with her head, and while I did my best to soothe her, I've never felt so fucking useless in my entire life. She cried for a while before she drifted into an uneasy sleep. I don't want to wake her, but I need to get up for the meet with Howard.

That fucker dies today.

He has no idea my woman has the support of a motorcycle club at her back, and he's going to pay for everything he's done or said.

The shit he spouted on the phone to her made me sick to my fucking stomach. Hearing it pissed me off. I'm going to carve his fucking mouth up for spewing that shit at her.

Carefully, I pull the covers back and slip out of the bed.

I'm not careful enough though, because I hear a sleepy, "Matt?"

"Sorry, babe. I didn't want to wake you."

She sits up, the blanket sliding down her body to reveal dusky pink nipples. Her tits are growing all the time, but this morning they look bigger again. I sink onto the edge of the bed, reaching out and palming her nearest tit, unable to stop myself. Elyse meets my eyes as I do, letting out a little gasp of pleasure.

"I wish I had time to make love to you right now, babe, but I have to go."

She has no idea how much I wish I could stay. I don't want to leave. I want to bury myself balls deep in her pretty cunt for the rest of the morning.

I settle for stroking my thumb over her nipple instead.

"Howard," she murmurs.

"Don't say that cunt's name," I growl. Especially not while I'm holding her breast.

"Sorry. That's where you're going though, isn't it? You're meeting him."

"Yeah." I dip my head, slanting my mouth, and capture her lips. She tastes like fucking sunshine. The light to my dark. The heat to my cold. The love of my life. I'll do anything for her.

Anything.

"I love you," I tell her, meaning every word of it.

"I know. I love you too," she says back. "Please be careful. He who can't be named is dangerous."

"So am I."

"Matt."

I kiss her again. "I'll be careful," I promise. "I'll have my brothers at my back. Don't worry about me."

I thread my fingers through the hair at the side of her head as I pull her in for another kiss. This one is possessive as much as it's needy.

"By the end of today, this shit will be over," I tell her.

She huffs out a breath. "Okay."

"Go back to sleep."

She lies down, hugging the pillow to her. "Love you."

"Love you too."

I go into the bathroom and shower. The water wakes me up as I ready myself for what I'm going to do today. I've tortured men before. I'm not afraid to get my hands dirty. I was killing men before I was a man myself. I have no fear of carving Howard into strips.

But the need to have this over with burns through my gut. I need to know she and Aaron are safe.

When I'm clean, I step out, wrapping a towel around my waist, and head back into the bedroom. Elyse is out of it, curled on her side, her hand resting on top of the blankets where our baby is nestled. She's going to be an amazing mother. There's already nothing she wouldn't do for this baby.

I go into the walk-in and pick out my clothes. A pair of black jeans and a black tee. I also pack a spare pair of clothes into a holdall before I pull my kutte on.

The ride to the clubhouse feels like it takes forever. My bike, which usually soothes me, doesn't help me get out of my head this morning.

By the time I pull into my space outside the front

doors, my anger is at dangerous levels. Howler is leaning against the front wall, his booted foot resting against the brick, a cigarette hanging out of his mouth.

"You ready for this?" he asks.

I shove my hands in my pocket after dropping my holdall on the pavement in front of him. "Yeah, I'm ready."

It takes an hour to get everyone on the road to the meet. I'm twitchy as fuck by this point, but as I climb in the back of the van with my brothers, who are ready to throw down to protect my woman, I feel a calm come over me. I can do this.

I have to do this.

For Elyse.

For Aaron.

For my family.

The warehouse is an old mill building. It's red brick, with slatted windows, most of which are missing glass and part of the frames. The walls are littered with graffiti and nature is trying to reclaim a foothold, vines and weeds growing up the side of the building and in the cracks in the paving stones. Brew drops us off then drives off to hide the van. My brothers and I spread through the warehouse, which is desolate inside. There are still some of the old shelving units and crates littering the space, a few places to hide. We get into position and wait.

And wait.

The time to meet him comes and goes, and I get a really uneasy feeling in the pit of my stomach. Every instinct in my body is screaming at me to go home.

Howler, sensing my nerves, places a hand on my arm. "He'll be here."

"What if he doesn't come? Fuck, Howler, I got a real bad feeling here. Something is telling me to get home."

Howler doesn't answer straight away, then he says, "Call your girl."

I pull my phone out and pull up her contact details, hitting the call button. It rings and rings and rings.

That feeling in my stomach becomes a steel anvil, pressing down on my gut. Why ain't she answering?

I hang up and redial.

It rings out again.

Fuck.

I redial and get nothing again.

This time, I hang up and dial Aaron, hoping like fuck Elyse is just sleeping, but I know she isn't. There's no way in fuck she's sleeping that heavily that she can't hear my dialling her three fucking times.

As the call rings out, I start to feel desperation clawing at me.

"Something's wrong." I hang up, and then I'm moving. My brothers follow me.

"He doesn't know where she is, Blackjack."

As soon as I step outside and the cooler air hits me, I interlace my fingers behind my head and scream into the air, "Fuck!"

Howler grabs my arm, stopping me from pacing. "He doesn't know," he repeats. "How would he?"

I cast my mind through my memories, trying to think

of any moments that he might have had opportunity to figure out where she was.

It hits me like a fucking wrecking ball.

This is my fault.

"I went to the flat. He could have followed me. He could have fucking realised Elyse was with me! I have to get to her, now!"

Brew runs to get the van, moving faster than I've ever seen him. It still feels like it takes an eternity for him to return. When it skids to a stop in front of us, we all pile in.

The drive to my flat feels like it takes forever, and the entire way I keep ringing her phone. No one answers, and that pit in my stomach grows wider. Howard has her.

I know it in my gut.

I close my eyes, clasping my hands on top of my knees as I lean back against the wall of the van. Brew, give him his due, is driving like he's in NASCAR to reach the flat.

He stops suddenly. "We're here," he says, turning around in the driver's seat.

I stumble up, bending so I don't hit my head on the roof, and fumble to get the doors open. My hands are shaky, sweaty, and it's hard to get the locking mechanism to undo. Terror finally pulls it back for me, and I stagger out onto the street.

I'm barely aware of what I'm doing as I use the security fob to get into the building and take the stairs two at a time. My heart is hammering so hard in my chest I feel as if I can hear my blood roaring through my veins.

As I approach the flat, I know instantly something is wrong. The door is open just ever so slightly.

I grit my teeth as I push it with my foot. It swings open, and I see the chaos immediately. There's shit everywhere, as if there was a hell of a fight. I freeze for a second before my legs move again.

"Elyse!" I call her name as I move from room to room. There are more signs of destruction, of chaos. Whatever happened, she put up a hell of a fight.

Something catches my eye in the living room.

Blood.

It's on the carpet, a small patch of it. I move to in, crouching down, my head pulsing with a headache.

"She's gone," I say, my voice cracking as it chokes out of me.

Howler steps in behind me. "Yeah, let's go and get her back."

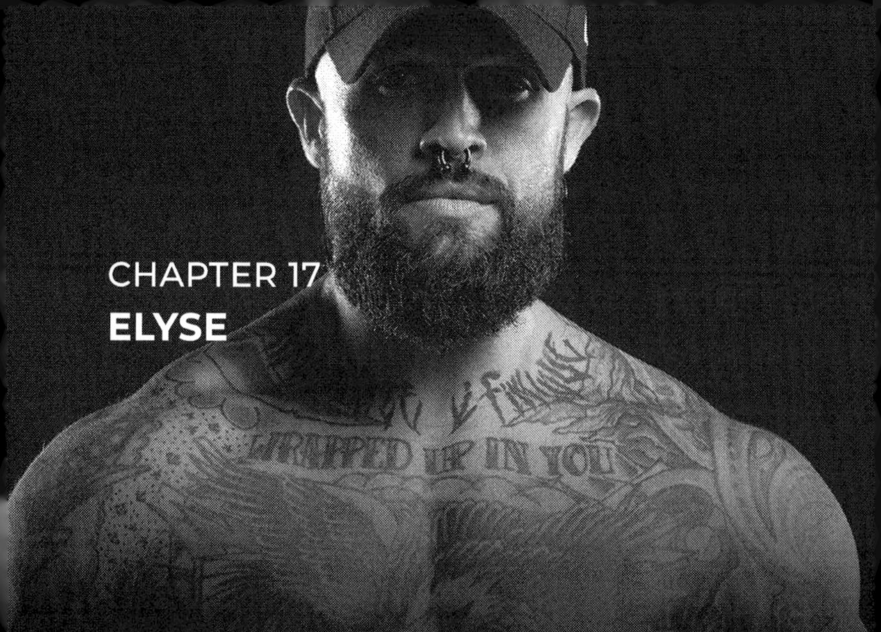

CHAPTER 17
ELYSE

When I wake, Matt is gone. I get up and throw up, as has become my routine, shower and pull on some leggings and a cropped sports bra. My boobs hurt, and they're the only thing I can wear without pain.

As I stand in the walk-in, I find myself looking in the full-length mirror, trying to work out if my belly is starting to protrude or if it's just bloat, as I've been telling Matt it is. I turn to the side, placing my hand above my belly button. Maybe? There's maybe a slight protrusion, but my belly is still pretty flat. I was skinny before I got pregnant, but Matt's always making me eat, so I have a little more meat on my bones now. It's not like I went hungry before—I always made sure there was money for food—but there were times with working both jobs that I'd miss a meal in the cross over between start and finish times. It was inevitable.

Matt sends me food when he's at the clubhouse sometimes, just to make sure I eat something.

Unable to see a hint of baby bump, I reach for one of Matt's hoodies and shrug it on. I like wearing his clothes. They make me feel close to him.

Unsurprisingly, the garment drowns me, but I love oversized sweaters. I dig my hands into the pockets and make my way to the living room. Aaron's sitting in front of the TV playing on Matt's console. Whatever the game is, it seems bloody.

"Are you sure you should be playing this?" I ask as I go to the fridge.

"Yeah. Everyone at school plays it."

I roll my eyes. "It looks violent."

"It's fine," he assures me.

I grab a bottle of orange juice and pour a glass. "Do you want something to eat?" I ask him.

"Uh, I'll have whatever you're making." He doesn't tear his gaze from the screen.

Sighing, I move to the cupboard to see what there is to eat. I find some bread and decide on toast. I'm still feeling a little queasy after throwing up this morning so it's probably not a good idea to have anything too heavy.

I shove four rounds of bread in the toaster and turn back to my brother, who still hasn't moved.

"Don't you have homework?"

"It's the weekend."

"That means you don't have homework?"

"Means there's always Sunday to do it."

"Well, you'd better. You've got biking this afternoon, right?"

"Yeah, Matt said he can't take me, but some dude called Ralph is."

Ralph is a prospect, and that isn't his real name, though I don't know why they call him Ralph.

The toast pops. I grab some butter from the fridge and spread it on all four pieces. Then I grab the chocolate spread for Aaron. He's addicted to it. I spread it on his pieces and cut them in half before I carry both plates over.

"Put the game down and eat," I say.

He grumbles, but he does pause it to take the toast from me. "You need to eat more," he says.

"I'm eating the same as you."

He takes a bite of his toast. "Yeah, but you're pregnant."

I narrow my eyes. "Has Matt been talking to you?"

Aaron shifts his shoulders. "He says we need to take care of you, and I agree. No one ever takes care of you, so me and him have to." His eyes raise and meet mine. "You deserve to be looked after too."

My throat feels like it clogs up suddenly, emotion choking me. "Okay, you can't say shit like that to me, not unless you want me to snotty cry on you."

He wrinkles his nose. "Ugh, eating."

I smile. "You're a good kid, Aaron. I'm sorry I haven't always been able to provide for you."

He snaps his gaze towards me. "Are you kidding? You've done everything for me. I never felt wanted until you took me in, Elyse. I love you."

"I love you too, and you know no matter what happens, you'll always have a home with me and Matt."

He nods and takes a bite of his toast. "Matt's told me that."

"Mouth closed, animal. And he has?"

"Yeah." He swallows. "We talk all the time."

"About what?"

"Mostly about you and bikes."

I cock a brow. Nice to know I'm in the same sphere as bikes.

A knock on the door has both our heads whipping in that direction. No one ever knocks on the door—well, the occasional delivery person if they manage to get through the main doors of the building. It drives Matt crazy that residents hold the door open for delivery people.

"I bet Matt's sent us breakfast," I say, smiling. I don't want Aaron scared of his own shadow. We're safe here. No one knows we're living with Matt. "We should have held off on the toast, right?"

I push up, sliding my plate on the coffee table. As I walk down the hallway towards the door, unease suddenly prickles through me. I don't know what it is, but I feel suddenly uncertain, so much so that I pause.

I'm being stupid.

We're safe, I repeat.

I wish the door had a peephole, but the building's access is controlled by video intercoms so there's not one on the front door. No one is supposed to get in without using the intercom.

Slowly, I unlock the door, and as soon as I open it a

crack, weight presses against it. It shoves the door open, forcing me back. I hit the wall behind me, the coats and jackets on the wall rack softening my fall.

A hand is suddenly wrapped around my throat, and I'm looking into Howard's eyes.

They blaze with rage as he tightens his grip so hard I can't breathe past his hold. Fear, panic and desperation has me clawing at his hold, trying to pull him off me, but he's stronger than me.

Holding my throat, he drags me into the living room. Aaron comes to his feet, his eyes flaring.

"Let go of her!" He tries to fight Howard, but he's a kid, and when Howard slams a fist into the side of his head, my brother staggers, going down to his knees.

"Stop." I gasp out the word, but it's all I manage.

Howard pulls me into him, heat blazing through him. "Did you really think I was stupid enough to fall for your shitty plan?"

He shoves me back, and I throw out my hands to cushion myself as I go down heavily. My head catches the corner of the coffee table, and for a moment I see stars.

My hand comes up to my face, feeling something warm dripping down it. There's blood on my fingers. Shit.

I blink rapidly, trying to clear my vision as Howard paces in front of us. I glance towards my brother, who is glaring at him through gritted teeth.

"You honestly think I haven't kept tabs on you from the moment you smashed my head in? I watched your flat, night and fucking day. I saw your biker come poke around and leave." He tears his fingers through his hair. "I knew you were with the Sons. I knew that call yesterday was a trick to get me there. Seems I'm fucking smarter."

He strides over to me and grabs my arm, dragging me up. I yelp at the tightness of his grip on my bicep. "I told you, bitch. Your cunt is mine. Just because you gave it to some fucking prick biker, doesn't change a thing."

He drags me out into the hallway. Aaron staggers after him, clawing at him, hitting him. Doing anything he can to protect me. It's hopeless. My brother is smaller and weaker than a grown man.

"Kid, I will slit your fucking throat if you don't stop."

"Aaron, stop," I gasp out.

My brother's helpless eyes come to me. I try to send him a message with my eyes. Stay alive. Stay safe.

"You can't just take her," Aaron argues.

"You have no idea what I can do."

"The Sons will kill you for this!" Aaron spits out.

Howard stops and turns back to him. "If I was scared of those little leather-wearing pricks, do you think I'd be here?"

That makes my stomach flip. Why isn't he scared? He should be. The Sons have a huge reach.

Howard slams his fist into my brother's face again, making him stagger back against the wall.

"Stop hitting him!" I scream at Howard, fear for my brother overcoming all sense.

Howard fists his fingers in my hair, dragging my head back. "Maybe I should just kill the little shit."

"No, please, no. Don't hurt him."

"Then come with me. Quietly."

I try not to think about my baby as I nod. I will do whatever I have to in order to protect him or her, but I can't throw my brother to the wolves either.

"Okay. Just… leave him alone."

"I don't want your brother. Just you."

His words make cold run through me, but I nod. "I'll come. Aaron, stay here."

"No fucking way—"

"Stay here!" I scream at him. It's the first time I've ever raised my voice to him, and he recoils back, his eyes narrowing.

He's the only shot I have of help finding me. I need him to raise the alarm. I need him to step up and save me.

I let Howard drag me out into the corridor and down the stairs. I stumble on a few because of his pace, but his hold on me helps to keep my balance. My heart is hammering, my mouth is dry. I feel nauseous, and I know it's not morning sickness. This is real primal fear. He's going to rape me and then kill me.

That surreal thought rolls through my brain as he drags me over to a car parked outside the building. It's a large four by four thing that looks more like a tank than a vehicle. It's about to become my prison. He opens the back door and pulls out a pair of handcuffs.

"Hands behind your back."

My blood freezes, but fear he will go back upstairs and carry out his threat of killing my brother makes me do as he commands. He clamps the metal around my wrists and then shoves me.

"In the car."

I climb in, my centre of gravity wrong with my hands behind my back as they are. As soon as I'm sitting, he closes the door and climbs into the front seat. The engine rumbles to life, and the car moves away from the kerb. Matt's face flashes across my vision. He's never going to find me.

I turn to look out of the back window, and I see my brother running after us. Fuck! My heart races. Don't see him… don't see him.

I hold my breath until we turn the corner and I lose sight of him.

I turn back to look out of the front windscreen. "Where are you taking me?" I ask quietly.

"Don't talk," he growls.

I close my mouth and take a shaky breath. My stomach churns savagely. My only thought is keeping my baby safe until Matt can find me.

And I have no doubt he will find me.

He'll not rest until he does.

We don't drive for long, maybe ten minutes. We're in a part of the city that is run by smaller gangs and has a reputation for being dangerous if you don't affiliate with the right one.

He pulls into a garage at the back of a row of terraced properties, and when the door shuts behind us, I feel hopelessness wash through me.

I'm never going to be found.

I have to do whatever I can to escape. To survive.

I know where I am, so that's something.

He should have blindfolded me. The fact he didn't doesn't make the churning in my gut lessen.

Howard climbs out of the car, shutting the door behind him. He comes to the back door and opens it. Grabbing my arm, he tugs me to make me come out. I don't fight him. My head is already throbbing, and I don't want to give him another reason to hurt me.

"You don't have to do this," I say as my feet touch the concrete floor of the garage.

He ignores me, shutting the door behind me and leading me over to a door that opens directly into the house.

I swallow down the bile creeping up my throat. The house is nice. Well decorated, clean. It doesn't look like somewhere a murder takes place.

Is this his home?

For some reason, that doesn't make me feel any relief.

He pulls me through the kitchen and into a small living room before ordering me up the stairs.

This is it.

This is the moment he's going to rape me.

I steel myself, trying to keep calm. I can do this. I can get through this. I can survive. My baby can survive.

At the top of the stairs, there are two doors either side. He pulls me into the first room and flicks on the light. There's a divan with a mattress on top. No sheets. The window is covered in black paper, meaning I can't see out.

Shivers race up my spine and my gut churns savagely. "Get on the bed," he orders.

I shake my head. "Please don't."

"The bed. Now."

"Howard, I didn't lie. I am pregnant. Please don't hurt me or my baby."

He fists his fingers into my hair and yanks my head back. "I don't give a fuck that you let that dirty biker come inside you."

He keeps hold of my hair as he uses his other hand to grab the waistband of my leggings. Fear clutches my heart. I try to pull away, but this just makes my scalp burn. My hands aren't free to fight him, so I can do nothing as he pulls them down my legs.

"Howard, stop." The desperation in my voice does nothing to prevent him from shoving his hand inside my underwear.

The world feels like it stops as his fingers brush against my folds.

I think about Matt.

I think about Aaron.

I think about my baby.

I think about anything but the disgusting fingers stroking through my pussy. My breath tears out of me. My eyes fill with tears as he pushes his fingers inside me.

"I own this cunt," he says, his eyes filled with menace.

"No, you don't," I breathe the words.

Anger blazes through him. He pulls his fingers from my pussy and wraps both hands around my throat. Holding me, he shoves me back onto the mattress. Without my hands free, I go down heavily. He grips both my knees. I tense instantly, fighting him as he tries to part my legs. The look on his face is filled with such anger, such malice, it terrifies me. I sob and scream as I fight to keep my legs closed, but he's stronger. He pushes both my knees down, spreading me open.

"Stop," I cry.

He pulls my leggings further down my legs, my underwear following.

I try to fight, to close my legs again, but he's got a knee between them, stopping me.

This isn't happening.

This can't be happening.

Adrenaline floods my body as I fight for my life, using everything I have available to me. I kick my legs, I wriggle, I twist. Nothing stops him. He holds me down with his hand pressed against my throat while his free hand struggles to pull his pants down.

This time, there is no Aaron to save me.

No Matt.

I'm alone.

I close my eyes, and I try to breathe through tormented lungs.

"The fuck are you doing?"

The new voice has my eyes snapping open. I recognise it instantly. Howard half turns as a fist swings out and slams into the side of his face. He staggers back, releasing his hold on me.

My eyes shift to the large figure standing in the doorway, and for a moment, I think I'm hallucinating. It can't be him. It can't.

"She's fucking mine!" Howard roars.

"Are you crazy? This isn't what I signed up for. You

weren't to lay a finger on her." His eyes slide to me, taking in my pulled down pants. Shame burns through me at him seeing me like this. "Were you trying to *rape* her? You fucking pervert."

He hits Howard again, over and over. The two of them wrestle, slamming into the wall behind them as they fight hard, trying to destroy each other. I watch, my heart hammering. He gets Howard in a headlock and squeezes. Howard fights against him, clawing at his arms, but he's nowhere near as big as him. Howard succumbs, collapsing into a heap.

He straightens, breathing hard. There's blood streaming from his nose, but his eyes come to me.

I blink, and he doesn't disappear.

"I'm sorry, Elyse. I never meant for it to come to this."

He steps over to me, and I shift up the mattress, moving away as much as I can. A flash of hurt covers his face for a moment, but I don't care. I don't trust him. "I deserve that, but I swear, baby girl, I never meant for this to happen."

I stare at my father, my gut churning.

"Never meant for what to happen?" I whisper, an ugly feeling spreading through me.

"For you to get hurt. This wasn't part of it. You weren't to be touched." He moves over to Howard's downed body and searches his pockets. After a moment, he pulls out a small set of keys. "Let me… redress you."

"I don't want you to touch me."

He grimaces. "Baby girl—"

"Don't call me that! I'm not your baby or your girl. As far as I'm concerned, you're dead to me."

"I deserve that." He moves to my back, and I flinch as he undoes the cuffs. As soon as my hands are free, I pull my underwear and leggings back up and scramble off the bed, putting as much distance between us as I can.

"The debt?"

"Doesn't exist—not now anyway." I swallow bile as he sighs. "I was addicted to the horses, kid. I'm not proud to admit that. I did shit I would never have thought possible. I lost everything. Shit I worked a lifetime to build."

"So you used me to rebuild your life?" My voice sounds choked.

"Not just you." The admission makes my eyes close. "You were one of many we were getting money off." I'm going to puke. "For a while, I was paying back a bookie, but once that debt was cleared, I realised I could make even more money. Me and Jimmy were talking in the pub one night. We cooked up a plan."

"You both scammed me, made me believe I had no choice but to pay it. You made me think I would be killed!"

My father's eyes narrow. "You would never have been hurt!"

"Tell that to Howard, or Jimmy—whatever his fucking name is. He beat me. He forced me to do things I can never recover from, all so you could live your life?"

His face contorts. "What did he do to you?"

I step back as he steps towards me. "Stay away from me or I swear to god I will kill you."

Dad scrubs his fingers over his lips. "I'm sorry, kid."

"I scraped and worked two jobs to keep you and your prick of a friend in booze and horses?"

"You have that fancy office job. I thought—"

"You thought what? That you'd have your pal abuse me every week to get small change from your own fucking daughter?"

The hurt in my voice is undeniable. I knew my father hated me. I never realised how much until this moment.

He licks his lips. "This was never meant to happen."

I feel sick. "Just so you know, my fancy office job pays minimum wage. I was living hand to mouth while trying to take care of your son."

"We didn't need much. We have a few people we run through the scheme, getting money off each of you."

"You didn't need much? How did you expect me to find ten grand, twenty, fifty?"

His brows draw together. "It was supposed to be five hundred quid each month."

I laugh. "I'm guessing he never mentioned he got ten grand off me one month." Dad's face blanches. "There really is no honour amongst thieves, is there?"

"Where the fuck did you get ten grand from?"

"I screwed over a biker."

"What?"

"The vice president of the Untamed Sons. I was desperate. I went to a casino, caught his eye, slept with him, and stole his winning chips." I laugh. "He could have killed me. He should have. Do you know what he did? He let me go."

"Elyse... I never meant for that to happen. That wasn't my plan."

"Howard, or whatever his name is, wanted me, Dad. He knew I couldn't pay. Clearly, he made it so I couldn't just so he could abuse me. And you put this into motion. You sat and plotted and thought this was a good idea." I let out a sad breath. "I knew you hated me. Knew it. But I didn't know how much until this moment."

"I don't hate you—"

I snap my eyes to him. "Well I hate you! I never want to lay eyes on you again."

"Elyse—"

"No. You stay away from me. I can't do this with you."

"I'm not going to walk away."

"That biker I tricked—I'm now his old lady. You come near me, and I'll set him and the entire Untamed Sons club on you. I'll make sure they never find your fucking body. Stay away from me, stay away from Aaron."

I start to move to the door, but he grabs my wrist. "This isn't finished."

"Yeah, it is."

"No one is leaving." Howard's voice draws our attention. I see the flash of light as it hits the blade of the knife he's clutching between his fingers.

"Sit on the fucking bed," he orders.

My head feels dizzy.

"What the fuck are you doing?" Dad demands.

"On the bed!" he screams. Dad pushes me towards the bed. We both sit, my heart racing as I follow the knife. "You attacked me."

"You tried to rape my daughter."

"Well, now you're going to watch as I fuck her bloody."

"Over my dead body."

Howard smiles. "That can be arranged."

He lunges forward, the knife raised.

And my heart stops.

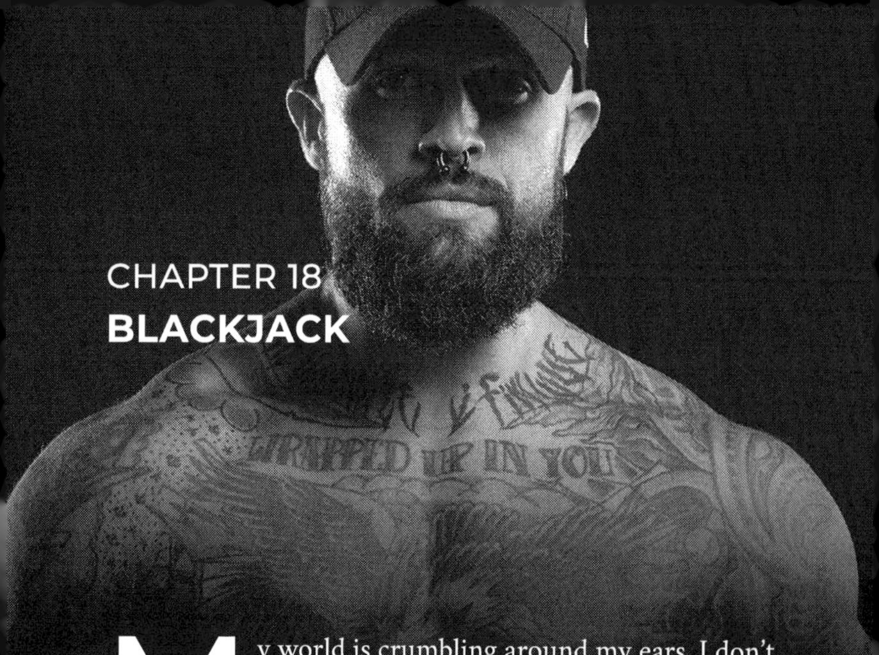

CHAPTER 18
BLACKJACK

My world is crumbling around my ears. I don't know what the hell to do. She's gone. Aaron too. There's blood. Every inch of my body feels cold.

Trick comes to me, holding his phone in his hand. "I got Rug on the line. Aaron's at the clubhouse."

"Fuck," I start for the door, but Howler stops me with an arm over my chest.

"Slow down. The kid's safe. Your woman ain't. Talk to the kid, find out what he knows."

Right.

I take the phone from Trick. "Aaron?"

"Hang on, I'll put him on," Rug says. Any animosity he might have towards me for punching him out in the middle of the clubhouse is not present as he speaks to me.

"Hello?" Aaron's voice sounds down the line. The kid sounds scared, but hyped.

"Hey, kid. You okay?"

"I didn't know where else to go. I didn't have my phone. I just panicked. I ran to the clubhouse. Howard took Elyse."

"You did good," I assure him. "We're going to get her back, I promise."

"I saw the car leave."

My stomach twists. "I'm sorry."

"No, I mean I saw it leave, Matt. I know the registration. I memorised it."

Fuck, my heart soars. If it's not stolen, we might have a chance of getting to the registered owner. It's worth a shot.

"Give it to me." I pull my phone out while I sandwich Trick's between my ear and shoulder so I can type the details.

Howler takes it from me and steps away, pulling his own phone out. He has contacts who can get him the name of who the car is registered to.

"Your sister, was she hurt?"

"She hit her head," Aaron says. "She was bleeding."

Fuck. I grind my teeth. "You stay at the clubhouse until we come back, okay?"

"He could have killed me. He didn't. Why?"

"I don't know."

"He's going to hurt her," he says quietly.

"Ain't going to let that happen."

"Bring her home."

"I will, kid." The line goes dead. I hand Trick back his phone as Howler comes off the phone.

"Car is registered to James Franklin." Is that Howard's

alias or an innocent person caught up in this shit? "Car ain't been reported stolen," Howler adds. "It could be his."

"He was smart enough to use an alias but not smart enough to use a car not registered to him?" Trick raises his brow.

"If it's him," I say.

"Let's check it out," Howler says. "Trick, Socket, stay here and see what else you can find out. There's CCTV on the building. It might help."

The brothers nod, giving me a sympathetic look as they walk away.

I scrub a hand over my face. Howler grips my shoulder, forcing my attention to him.

"Let's check out the address, see if she's there."

"Okay."

We head out to the van. Brew and Terror come with us —Brew driving.

I sit up front this time, while the others take the back of the van. My leg jiggles the entire drive over. I'm terrified for her, for our baby. This fuck who has her has already abused her; he's tried to rape her before. I hope we get there before any irreparable damage is done.

I close my eyes and take a steadying breath. I need to focus on one thing and one thing only. Her.

I hold my anger for Howard—James—whatever the fuck his name is, at bay. There will be time to unleash my inner rage later.

Brew pulls into a sprawling housing estate. It's run down, though the houses look like they were built in the seventies or early eighties. The cars are mostly old, the front gardens clean and tidy on some properties but unkempt on others.

I stare out the side window, trying to get a feel for it.

Brew suddenly slams on the brakes, and I nearly catapult through the windscreen. It's only my seatbelt that keeps me from shooting out of my seat. Behind me, I hear cursing from my brothers, but my attention goes to the front window. Running barefoot up the road is my beautiful redhead.

She's running like she has the devil on her heels.

I'm out of the van before I contemplate the risk. My boots pound against the tarmac, and I hear my brothers behind me.

I can see the moment Elyse sees me. Her eyes widen, and the smile she gives me makes my heart thud.

"Bitch!" The screamed voice has my eyes sliding in the direction it came from.

A man is coming up behind her, a knife in his hand. He's bloodied, and the rage coming off him terrifies me.

Her footsteps falter. She stumbles and trips, crying out as she hits the tarmac.

Fuck, I'm not going to reach her in time. He's going to get to her before I can.

I pump my arms faster, propelling my legs forward as she staggers up. Come on, baby. Move.

I don't know how the fuck I do it, but I reach her just as he does, throwing myself between him and Elyse.

He slashes the knife down, catching my arm. It tears through the skin like it's going through butter.

I don't even feel the sting of the blade. I grab his wrist

and squeeze until he releases the knife with a cry. My army training snaps into place, years of hand-to-hand combat coming back to me like muscle memory.

I grab him around the neck, pulling him back against my body. I want to beat the fucker to a pulp, but right now, my focus is on subduing him as fast as possible so I can check on Elyse.

He claws at the arm pressed against his throat, but I don't stop squeezing until he goes limp in my hold. I drop him to the ground.

"Get him in the van," Howler says as I step over his body and go to Elyse. Howler has her behind him, keeping her safe.

Relief floods me as she steps around my president, my oldest friend. Her bottom lip wobbles, before she throws her arms around me, burying herself against my chest.

Fuck.

I hold onto her like I'm scared to let her go. I pull her tight against my chest, my hand pressing into the back of her head to hold her against me. The relief at having her in my arms, safe, whole, is unmeasurable.

I didn't think this would happen.

I was so fucking scared I'd lose her. I kiss her hair, needing to feel her as she sobs against my chest.

"Babe," I speak softly, trying to pull her back, needing to see her face. "Are you hurt? You took quite a spill."

She lifts her hands, showing me her palms. They're scraped and oozing blood.

"Fuck." They don't look deep, but they do look sore.

"We need to find Aaron."

"He's at the clubhouse. Ran right there after you were taken to get help."

She lets out a relieved breath. "I was so worried."

"Kid did good. He's the reason we found you. The guy who took you used his own car."

She snorts. "I'm not surprised. He's apparently not a career criminal. Just a dick trying to get money."

"He's Howard?"

"Yeah. Or Jimmy. He's friends, or associates, with my father. He was behind this."

"Who?"

"My father. He orchestrated all of this."

My jaw tightens. "Fuck."

"Elyse." At the voice, I pull my woman behind me, protecting her as an older man limps up to us. He's bloody, a long gash to his side that is oozing blood rather than pouring it.

"I've got absolutely nothing to say to you," she hisses at him.

"Your father?" I ask. She nods. I glance at Terror, who steps towards him.

"Wait!" Elyse says. "He tried to help me."

"He's also the reason you're here in the first place."

She gives me a sad smile. "I can't deny that, but he did try to save my life, Matt. That counts for something."

"Ain't helping that cunt."

"I'm not saying take him home and patch him up, but he fought Howard so I could escape. I know he's a bastard, but I don't want his death on my conscience."

I stare at my beautiful woman, wondering how she can have so much compassion for someone who hurt her.

"Babe."

"Please, Matt."

"Fine." I turn to her father. "I lay eyes on you again and I'll cut your throat."

"She's my daughter. You can't keep me away."

I round on him, keeping Elyse behind me still. "She's fucking nothing to you." I turn back to Elyse. "Going to pick you up."

"Okay."

I sweep her up into my arms bridal-style, so she doesn't have to walk across the tarmac again. I don't want her feet getting more cut up than they are.

"What about Jimmy?" her father asks.

"Not your business."

"Son," he says.

"Ain't your son."

He rubs a finger over his lip. "You take care of my daughter."

"I intend to."

"And make it hurt. Whatever you're planning on doing to Jimmy, don't go easy on him." He ducks his head. "For what it's worth, Elyse, I'm fucking sorry."

"Your apology isn't worth shit. Stay away from me and Aaron."

I turn and walk back to the van. She nestles against my chest, her head tucked into my shoulder.

When we reach the van, my brothers have Howard in the back. I put Elyse in the front and slide in next to her. I pull her seatbelt on, clipping it in place before I do my own. She looks tired.

"You're bleeding," she says.

I glance down at the cut to my arm. It isn't too deep, but it is dripping blood. I lean forward and grab the first aid kit from the glove box. She opens it, tucking her hair behind her ears as she searches for what she wants to use. I sit still while she places gauze on my cut and tapes it down. It's not neat, but it does the job.

"I'm sorry you got hurt," she says when she's done.

"I'd take a thousand cuts to keep you safe." I cup her face and lean my head against her forehead.

She breathes deeply. "I knew you'd come," she whispers.

"I'll always find you, Elyse."

The trust she has in me makes me want to fucking kiss her all over. She settles into my side. Her arm wraps around my waist. "I love you."

"I love you too, babe."

I glance over my shoulder as Brew starts the van up. My brothers have Howard on the floor of the van, hogtied. Retribution rushes through my bloodstream, heated and violent. I'm going to enjoy every second with him.

"Back to the clubhouse?" Brew asks.

I shake my head. "Drop us at the hospital first."

Elyse glances up at me. "That's not necessary. I'm okay."

"I want to make sure." I kiss her head. "Just humour me, okay?"

She huffs out a breath. "Okay, but there's no need."

"Then we'll be in and out."

Brew drives us to the hospital. I hold Elyse against me the entire way, as if I'm scared to let go of her. Truthfully, I am. I feel like she'll disappear if I do.

Brew stops in the drop off circle outside the main entrance to the emergency department.

I carry her inside, leaving my brothers to handle Howard until I get back. The nurse at the desk glances up as we approach, taking in my woman and her bare feet and the cut to her head. I can see the thought process she has instantly as she notes my kutte.

I did this.

"I need someone to look at my wife. She's pregnant. She tripped over, cut her head and hands."

The nurse forces a smile. "I need to take some details first."

"Put me down, Matt," Elyse says softly.

I lower her onto the floor, unable to stop from kissing her head as I do. Fuck, I wish we were home so I could hold her.

Elyse gives the nurse the details she asks for.

"How many weeks pregnant are you?"

"Eleven weeks. Nearly twelve."

"Any spotting, bleeding or cramping?" Elyse shakes her head. "Okay, take a seat. Someone will call you through soon."

I lead her over to two chairs and we sit. "You warm enough?" I ask. She's in just a tee and leggings.

"I'm okay," she says, leaning her head against my shoulder. I wrap my arm around her, pulling her closer.

"I was fucking terrified when I realised what that cunt did," I admit. "I'm fucking sorry, Elyse. That fucker shouldn't have got within an inch of you."

She peers up at me. "You couldn't have known he'd do that."

"I promised you nothing would touch you."

Her eyes close for a second. "I'm safe and I'm breathing. Our baby too. That's all that matters, Matt."

Fuck, the simplicity of that statement doesn't take into account the terror I've been feeling since I learnt she was taken. She was only gone for a short time, but it felt like a hundred years.

We sit together, her head on my shoulder, until we're called through. The doctor does a thorough examination. He cleans the scrapes to her hands. The cut to her head is mostly closed now, but he wants to do a scan just in case. Elyse lies like a pro when the doc asks how she did it. She's so convincing even I find myself questioning if what happened really did.

"Your blood pressure looks better than last time you were here."

"He's taking good care of me," she says, nudging my arm. The doc smiles.

"I can tell."

"Is my baby okay?"

"Let's do a scan, just to check, but I'm not worried."

"It's not going to be an inside thing again, is it?" Elyse

asks, wrinkling her nose. I don't know what the inside thing is, but it sounds uncomfortable.

"We should be able to see something with a routine ultrasound."

She blows out a relieved breath, and I squeeze her hand.

"I'll be back with the machine," the doc says before ducking around the curtain. The noise of the emergency department fades into the background as I stare down at Elyse on the trolley.

With my other hand, I brush her hair back from her face. "You doing okay?"

"Nervous."

"Yeah, babe, me too."

She frowns. "You are?"

"Ain't done this before either, you know?"

"What if the baby got hurt? I was careful. I did everything I could, but—"

I kiss her, silencing her fears. "Whatever happens, you took care of our baby, Elyse. I know that."

I have no doubt she defended herself and that she did everything to protect our kid.

The curtain opens and the doc comes back in with a machine on wheels. He sets it up on the opposite side of the trolley.

"Just pull your pants down a little and lift your top please."

Elyse lets go of my hand to do what is asked, exposing her belly. I take a steadying breath as she reaches for me again. My fingers intertwine with hers as the doc squirts some liquid on her stomach and pushes a probe against her belly.

"We should hear your baby's heartbeat and be able to see him or her quite clear on the scan," he says.

I stare at the screen as it ripples and moves in black and white. It looks like a load of static, nothing tangible. Then he stops, and a shape that could be a baby appears among the static.

"That's your baby."

Elyse squeezes my hand. My throat feels clogged suddenly as I stare at the blob of shapes on the screen. That's my kid. That thing that looks like a fucking kidney bean.

The doc presses buttons as he moves the probe around. "Baby's measuring great for eleven weeks. Everything looks good. I can't see any problems."

"Shouldn't we hear the heartbeat?" Elyse asks.

"Hang on." The doc presses something on the ultrasound machine and moves the probe. Suddenly, the cubicle is filled with a whomp-whomp-whomp sound. It feels like the floor beneath me shifts.

I haven't cried since I was a kid, but right now, my eyes are burning. "Fuck."

The doc laughs. "Yeah, it's pretty amazing, isn't it? It never gets old doing scans."

He prints out the image from the machine and hands it to Elyse. She stares at it, swiping at the tears rolling down her cheeks. "Look what we made."

"I know, babe. It's perfect."

"Do you know what the sex is?"

The doc glances at the screen. “Looking at it, I’d guess a boy, but it’ll be clearer at your twenty weeks scan. It’s not always easy to tell this early on so don’t go decorating the nursery just yet.”

A boy.

My brain feels like it short circuits.

I’m having a son?

I kiss her head. I want to thank her for giving me this gift, but I can’t choke the words out. Instead, I just say, “Love you.”

“Love you too.”

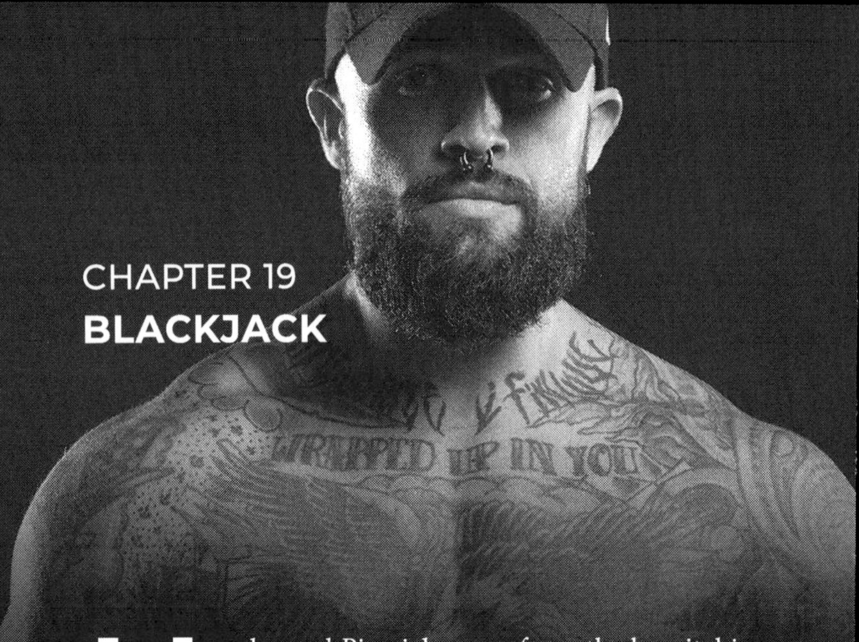

CHAPTER 19
BLACKJACK

Howler and Pia pick us up from the hospital in her car. Elyse is quiet on the drive home. She's exhausted. I don't know what happened to her when she was alone with Howard—she hasn't really opened up yet. I'm hoping she'll tell me at some point if it was something bad, but she seems calm and relaxed, which makes me feel the same way.

She leans against the side window, her eyes closed as the car heads in the direction of home.

"Thanks for picking us up," I say to them both.

Pia waves this off. "Of course we picked you up." She glances in the rear-view mirror at Elyse's sleeping form before returning her attention to the road. "How's she doing?"

"She's strong, keeping it together. We, uh… we saw our baby." Saying that is fucking surreal.

Prez twists to look at me, grinning. "Fuck, man, that's amazing."

Yeah, it is. I'm still reeling from it. It looked like a blob, but I could sort of make out the baby shape if I squinted.

"You'll be a wonderful father," Pia tells me.

"Ain't sure about that, considering the violence blazing through me right now," I tell her. While we were at the hospital waiting to be seen, I spoke to Aaron. The kid was freaked about his sister and about the entire situation. Mara checked him over because Howard clocked him in the face. That shit pissed me off. He's a kid. How does a fucking grown man hit a kid? "What happened to that prick anyway?"

I lost track of things while I was getting Elyse seen to at the hospital.

Howler glances at his old lady before twisting to look at me. "Terror's entertaining our guest."

Pia shifts in the seat, but keeps her eyes locked on the road. She's a good woman, loyal, and knows her place in the club. A lot don't, or don't like it when they get there. Not everyone is built ready for this world.

I snort. I know what Terror's idea of entertainment looks like. He has an assortment of sharp and pointy things at his disposal, and he's adept at using them all. Terror has a gift for keeping a person on the edge of consciousness, pushing the body to its limits without breaking it.

"I hope he's not having too much fun." I want to play with Howard or Jimmy too. I want to make that fucker cry like a baby.

"You'll get your turn," Howler assures me as Pia pulls into the parking area under my building. Once she parks in one of my assigned spaces, I get out of the car and walk around to Elyse's side.

As I open the door, she stirs. "Are we here?"

I push her hair off her face, hating how vulnerable she seems right now, but loving that she allows herself to be that way with me. She trusts me. That means more than words can say. "Yeah, babe. I'm going to carry you in."

"I can walk." The hospital gave her disposable slippers, but they don't have a sole on them, so I don't trust them to protect her feet. She's also barely awake.

"You're exhausted."

"I can still walk."

"Let me take care of you."

She sighs but relents. "Okay."

I pick her up and carry her to the lift while Pia and Howler lock the car and follow me.

As the lift moves up to our floor, all I can think is that I have my entire life in my arms. I don't know what the fuck I would have done if she'd been hurt.

The lift opens on our floor and Prez moves ahead of me to knock on the front door. Mara's voice comes from the other side.

"Who is it?"

"It's us, Mara," Howler says back.

The sound of the lock pulling back seems loud. She opens the door slightly before opening it fully when she sees me standing there with Elyse in my arms.

Her eyes go to Elyse before sliding up to me. "I'm glad she's okay," she tells me, before stepping out of the way so we can come inside.

I have to walk through the living area to get to the bedroom. As soon as I step over the threshold of the room, Aaron is on his feet, crossing the carpet. He has a bruise forming on his jaw that makes me want to kill Howard even more than I already do.

I try not to let my anger slide on to my face. The kid looks shaken up as it is. "She's okay," I assure him. "She's tired. It's been a long day."

Aaron takes my words at face value, some of the tension easing from his shoulders. "I was scared," he admits.

"Me too," I say, "but she's okay. Doctors checked her out. She just needs to rest. I'm going to put her to bed, kid, then I'll come back, okay?"

Aaron nods, so I walk through to the bedroom. Elyse is out of it when I pull back the covers and slide her onto the mattress. She doesn't stir when I cover her or when I press a kiss to her head.

I leave the bedroom, pulling the door to so I can hear her if she needs me, and make my way back to the living area.

Pia and Mara are in the kitchen, heads together, talking. Howler is perched on the sofa while Aaron is pacing.

As soon as I step into his space, I pull him against my chest. He instantly wraps his arms around my back. "You did so good. Thank you."

"I didn't do anything," he disagrees.

"You got the license plate. We found her because of you."

"Oh."

I pull back, grabbing his face between my hands so he looks at me. "You saved your sister's life."

"I did?"

"Yeah. Me and Howler need to do something for a few hours. I need you to take care of Elyse while I'm gone."

"Yeah, of course."

"She's going to need you, kid."

The resolve on his face makes me smile. "I won't let you down."

"I know." I turn to Howler. "Ready?"

"Yeah."

He moves into the kitchen area and kisses Pia before she hands him her keys. Then we leave the flat. The ride down in the lift is silent, and he doesn't speak to me until we get into the car.

Before he puts the key in the ignition, he turns to me.

"You sure you want to do this?"

I stare at him as if he's lost his fucking mind. "Been dreaming about taking this fucker's life from the moment I found out what he did to my woman. That feeling ain't gone."

He doesn't say anything for a moment, then nods. "Okay then."

We head over to one of our abandoned properties not far from the clubhouse. Howler parks the car in the garage, away from unfriendly eyes, and we enter the building.

As soon as we do, I can hear the sound of flesh meeting flesh ringing out. Terror must be working him over.

I pick up my pace, eager to be involved in the beating.

Stepping through the door at the back of the building into a large cargo bay, I see Howard hanging from a hook attached to the ceiling. He's swinging on his shoulders, his toes skimming the concrete beneath him.

His chest is a mass of mottled purple—bruises—but other than that he looks intact. Terror didn't do too much damage, which I'm grateful for. I want to fuck this prick up.

Howard's eyes roll in my direction, and I see fear in them. I wonder if it's the same fear Elyse showed when he stuck his cock in her mouth without permission, when he tried to rape her.

I pull my kutte off my shoulders, my eyes never leaving Howard. Howler takes it from me as I step up to Terror's table of instruments. My brother grins at me.

"What do you feel like using?" he asks.

I pick up a serrated knife, twisting it and peering at the blade. "Ain't sure. What do you recommend?"

He hands me a blow torch. "Start with this."

I twist the knob on the side, lighting it up. Howard starts to thrash on his chains.

"No, please, don't!"

"Did Elyse beg you too?" I ask him.

"For what?"

"To stop ramming your tiny pencil dick into her mouth."

He blanches, trying to move away from me as I step up to him with the flame.

"She wanted it."

Anger flames through me. “Is that what you’ve told yourself?”

“It’s true.”

I press the flame against a spot on his stomach. The smell of burning flesh hits the back of my nose at the same time as Howard starts screaming. I hold it against him for longer than necessary before pulling it away.

He sags in the chains, his body limp, his chest heaving as he sucks in breaths.

I hope it hurt, cunt.

“She’s pregnant, with my fucking kid. You tried to rape my woman when she was pregnant.”

“I didn’t kno—”

I press the flame against another spot, and his shrieks ring out. It’s the sweetest fucking symphony to my ears. I want him to suffer. She was so scared she hadn’t protected our baby. Her guilt will stay with me for a long time. So this prick isn’t getting to walk away unscathed.

“Please stop,” he begs when I pull the flame away.

“It’s not nice, is it? Losing control. Having your choices taken away.”

“That’s not what I did.”

“You fucked her mouth. She probably begged you to stop too. Did you just keep shoving yourself inside her? Did you care about her comfort as she choked and sobbed for you to end it?”

“I…” His voice hitches. “I’m sorry.”

“Your apology isn’t worth shit,” I tell him, directing the flame at his skin again.

Over and over, I burn him, listening to his screams. I

change to a knife when I get bored with that instrument. I cut his skin into flaps until blood coats every inch of him.

He's flagging. I can tell. His head is hanging impossibly low between his shoulders, his weight completely on his arms. He hasn't said a word in a while. Not even screams. This is going to be over soon, and I need him to suffer one last thing.

I step forward and fist my fingers in his hair, lifting his head. "You are a piece of shit, but you get to die knowing she'll live on, happy, healthy and taken care of. No one will give a shit that you're dead. No one will mourn you or even look for you. You're nothing. You'll always be nothing."

His rheumy eyes try to focus on me, but the pain in them clouds his focus.

I grab his cock in one hand. "You're never going to put your dick anywhere it isn't wanted again," I say.

Then I slice.

He screams. This isn't like the noises he made before. It's bloodcurdling.

When I'm done, I toss his cock on the floor, and then I look into his eyes.

"You're a cunt."

I stab him through the eye, right into his brain. He sags in his restraints, his body going dead weight as the life leaves him.

Covered in blood, I step back and drop the knife on the table. I feel drained. Exhausted, but righteous. Elyse got her vengeance. It won't take away her trauma, but at least that cunt can never touch her again.

Terror watches me carefully. Howler too.

"You did good, brother," Terror tells me.

I nod and walk into the room off this one. There's a hose and drain in the middle of the floor. I strip all my clothes off, tossing them into the bin bag left near the door. All our clothes will be burnt, along with this fucker's body.

I use the hose to sluice the blood from my body, washing every inch of my skin clean. When I'm done, I grab a towel from the chair in the corner and wrap it around my waist. There are hooks on the wall and a change of clothes hanging there. My brothers are always taking care of me.

I change into them and step back into the room when I'm done. Howard is still hanging there, dripping blood. I snarl at him before turning back to Howler and Terror.

"Get back to your woman. We'll take care of clean up."

I shake my head. "There's something I need to do first."

Howler gives me a questioning look. "What?"

"I need to talk to Elyse's father."

"Ain't going alone."

"Ain't scared of that cunt," I say. "I can handle one old man."

"Still ain't going alone. I'm coming." He turns to Terror. "You got this?"

"Yeah, Prez."

I glance at Terror. "Thank you."

He grins, showing perfectly straight white teeth. "Most fun I've had in a while, brother."

Howler pats Terror's chest and we head for the door.

"Feel better?" Howler asks as we make our way back to the garage.

"No," I admit. "He's dead, but it doesn't change what he did to Elyse."

"No, it doesn't, but she'll heal every day a little more. Pia has. She has setbacks, nightmares, but she's stronger than ever."

Pia was brutally raped for months.

"How do you ever let go of the anger for those fuckers?"

"I don't, but knowing they're dead fucking helps."

We get into the car and make the drive to the address where we found Elyse. I have no idea if that fucker will still be there, but I'm hopeful.

"Elyse will recover," Howler says, glancing between the road and me as he drives.

"I know. Just hate that she went through it at all. I should have done better. Been better."

"You can't worry about the past. It's happened. That fucker will never have the chance to hurt her again. You've given her that security."

"I know."

I did. It didn't make it easier to bear though.

Neither of us speak until we pull up outside the house. We get out of the car and walk towards the property. It doesn't look like anyone's home, but I go through the back gate into the yard, passing the garage. I try the back door and it opens. I glance at Howler, nodding. He pulls a knife from his pocket, flicking it open as we step inside.

The house is quiet.

I make my way through, but there's no sign anyone is here. I start up the stairs, Howler behind me. I'm on edge, ready for anything. I shove one of the doors at the top of the stairs open. The room is empty, so I move to the other. I find a room with a bare mattress inside it. The window is blocked with black paper. Elyse's father is sitting against the wall, his legs thrown out in front of him.

His eyes are red, his face drawn. He looks fucking pitiful. He shifts his gaze in my direction. "Decided to kill me?" he asks.

"You'd deserve it for what you did," I say.

"I can't even deny that," he agrees.

I scrub a hand over my face as I peer down at this pathetic specimen. "Howard's dead."

"Howard?"

"Jimmy… whatever the fuck his name is."

"Oh."

"Whatever fucking scheme you two were in, stops."

"Yeah, that's done," he says. His eyes go to the bed. "I walked in on him…" He buries his head in his hands. "I never wanted her hurt like that. Never."

My stomach fills with ice, my neck feeling clammy. "He rape her?" I ask the question that burns through me.

He shakes his head. "No, he got her undressed, but I stopped it before it got that far."

I let out a breath that feels lodged in my chest. "The fact you tried to help her is the only reason you're still breathing. That and her. She doesn't want you hurt. If it was down to me, you'd be breathing your last."

His eyes come to me. Haunted eyes. "I never meant for my daughter to be hurt like this. I trusted Jimmy."

"Yeah, well you put your trust in the wrong prick." I shake my head, trying to push the growing rage down. "You stay away from Elyse and from Aaron. You come near them, and I don't care what Elyse wants. I'll destroy you and bury you in the deepest hole I can find."

"You don't have to worry about me," he assures me. "I'm not going to go near either of them. I've fucked up their lives enough."

I turn to Howler. "Let's go."

Howler nods, and we head out of the house. My only thought is on getting back to my woman and making sure she, my kid, and Aaron have the best fucking life I can give them.

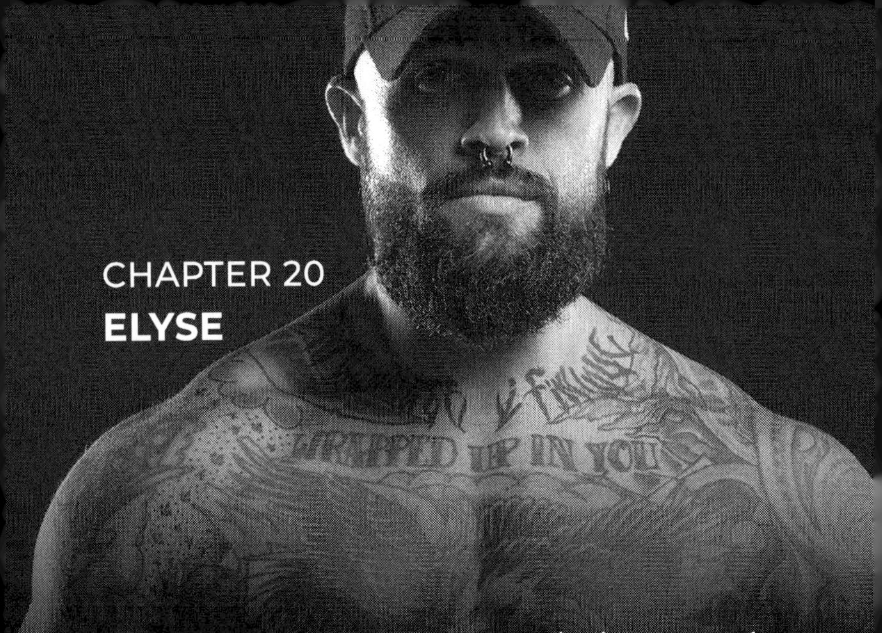

CHAPTER 20
ELYSE

I stare at my body in the mirror. I'm fourteen weeks pregnant and there's a definite baby bump there. It's like it just appeared overnight. I run a hand over my stomach, feeling the slope of it, completely obsessed with stroking my hands over it.

"Babe, are you—" Matt stops in the doorway of the walk-in. He takes me in, standing there in just my underwear, turned to the side, but it's not my lack of undress that has his attention. His eyes are locked on my belly as he steps towards me, and as soon as he's close enough, he runs a hand over my stomach. The loving way he does it makes my knees feel weak. He's everything I could have wanted from a man, and more. "That wasn't there yesterday," he observes.

It wasn't, though it has been sticking out a little more each week, but nothing really noticeable. I was starting to think my baby bump was never going to show up, but it's definitely there this morning.

"He's letting us know he's in there," I say, rolling to my toes so I can kiss him. The soft leather of his kutte shifts across my skin as he pulls me to him, deepening the kiss.

"You look beautiful," he tells me.

"I feel it," I admit.

"I want to fuck you," he says.

I meet his eyes, mine heated. "Then fuck me."

He hoists me into his arms and carries me into the bedroom. Gently, as if I'm made of glass, he lowers me onto the bed and parts my thighs.

"I'm not going back to work," I say as he goes between my legs.

Matt glances up, his brows cocking. "You want to talk about his now? While I'm about to stick my face in your cunt?"

His crassness makes me wince. "Honey."

He strokes a finger over my underwear, and I widen my legs to give him better access. "You want me to be prim and fucking proper? Say that I'm going to lick your vagina?"

I cover my face with my hands. "That's worse."

"Babe." He pulls my hands from my face so I'm looking into his eyes. "I don't give a shit if you work or you don't. That choice is and will always be yours, but I don't want to talk about this right now. I want to eat your pussy and then fuck you."

He palms my breasts, which are growing faster than my stomach, and I gasp. The books say they will get sensitive as my pregnancy develops, but sometimes it's almost close to a bite of pain when he touches them. He's careful not to go too hard, knowing this.

I watch as he moves between my legs and slides my underwear down before he drops them on the floor. He gives me a smirk before he buries his head in my pussy.

I gasp as he licks me like I'm his favourite meal. Each lick, each swipe of his tongue, is like heaven. My chest feels tight, like my heart might stop if I don't draw more air into my lungs. I try to suck in breaths as he rolls his tongue over my clit over and over until my legs are trembling.

I grip the sheets, trying to ground myself as my orgasm continues to build. Then he hits the right spot, the perfect one.

"Yes," I gasp. "There. Just there."

He intensifies ~~his~~ licking around the area, and I tense my thighs, trying not to crush his head as I shatter. My orgasm tears through me like wildfire. It burns every inch of my skin as I arch my back off the bed.

Fuck. I can't breathe. My lungs ache and my body feels so hot its almost uncomfortable. My pussy contracts and clenches savagely.

"All this wetness for me." He presses his nose into my pussy, making me twitch. I'm sensitive still from the orgasm still working through me. I grab his head, not sure if I want to pull him away or shove him deeper into me.

"Always for you," I tell him.

"Babe. Fuck." His hand skims over my stomach, feeling the slope where our baby is growing. "You gave me the best gift anyone could ever give me."

I smile. "I can't wait to meet our son."

He bends down and kisses my stomach, just below my belly button. "He'll be here before you know it."

Matt straightens, and the sound of his belt jingling makes me come up on my elbows to watch him undress. I never get tired of seeing this man naked. He removes his boots, his jeans and his underwear. Then he shrugs out of his kutte before he pulls his tee over his head. I let my eyes run over his tattooed body, my mouth dry. Matt is beautiful. It seems like the wrong word to use to describe a man as dangerous as he is, but there's a calm to his chaos. One he lets me be a part of.

He climbs back on the bed, his knees pressed into the mattress between my legs. I reach out and stroke his cock, the silky feel of it soft against my palm.

"I love you," I tell him.

"I love you," he says back. "More than you know."

In one swift movement, he enters me, pushing deep inside me. I groan as my pussy feels full of him. Clinging to his back, I try to pull him onto me, but he keeps his weight off me as he slides back to the tip before plunging back inside.

Every stroke feels amazing, like he's hitting so deep inside me, filling that emptiness that only he can. He fucks me hard, shoving me up the mattress with each thrust. I relax, taking him completely as he slams into me over and over.

I watch his face, my eyes locked to his as he loves on me in every way a person can be loved. He's my rock, my world, and I can see in his eyes that I'm his.

He pushes into me, and his hips stutter as he spills inside me. I come a moment later as his hot seed fills me.

Fuck.

He gives me his weight for a moment, nuzzling into my neck. He feels good on top of me. I love how he envelops me with his body. He doesn't stay there long though. A few seconds later he rolls off me, his cock sliding free from my body, and pulls me on top of him. I burrow against his chest, loving every moment of this.

"Don't go to sleep," he says, chuckling.

"You tire me when you fuck me," I murmur, my eyes closed.

"Baby, we've got places to be this morning."

"Uh huh… should have thought about that before you did this."

He strokes his fingers down my bare spine. "Ain't got an inch of self-control around you."

"I like that though," I admit.

He kisses my hair. "Two minutes and then we need to get moving."

"Can't it wait?"

"You need to meet Pia and Mara, and I need to get your brother to the track."

Aaron has been getting steadily better at dirt biking racing, but it gives me palpitations every time he goes.

"Don't let him get hurt."

"Babe."

"I mean it, Matt."

"I'll do my best."

We lie for what is definitely longer than two minutes, but eventually he huffs out a breath. "We need to move."

"I don't want to."

"We can lie in tomorrow," he promises.

"Fine." I climb off him and head to the shower to wash myself. Matt joins me, his hands roaming over my body under the pretence of washing me. He gets out first, leaving me to finish cleaning his cum from my pussy.

I'm as quick as I can be, but when I get back into the room, he's already redressed. I dress in a pair of loose-fitting jeans with my favourite flip flops and a fitted tee.

I spend the afternoon with Mara and Pia at the clubhouse, and when my brother and Matt come to pick me up in the new car Matt bought to accommodate the baby, I'm ready to get home. Everything tires me lately. I'm waiting to get to the glowing part of my pregnancy.

When Matt approaches, I stand and let him pull me into his arms. "You feeling okay?" he asks.

"Better now." I glance around him to my brother. "How was practice?"

He grins. "Great."

I arch a brow. "That all I'm getting? Great?"

Aaron shrugs. "That's what it was."

I turn to Pia and Mara. "Thanks for this afternoon."

"Let's do a girls night next weekend," Pia says. "My place. I'll make Jake go out."

"Sounds good."

We leave the old ladies and head out to the car. "It's good to see you three getting on so well," Matt says.

"I like them both," I admit.

"You want to have one of those girly nights at ours, I'll go out for the night," he says.

"As long as you're back to sleep next to me."

He pulls me against him, kissing my temple. "Always."

"Gross," Aaron mutters. "PDA should be illegal."

"One day you'll have a woman on your arm, and you'll see," Matt says.

Aaron wrinkles his nose but doesn't argue it.

As Matt drives us home, I find myself drifting off. I'm so tired lately. I can barely keep my eyes open.

A hand on my thigh has me jolting. "We're home," Matt says, drawing me out of sleep.

"Shit, did I fall asleep again?"

"Babe, you're growing a person."

"I know, but I feel like I can't stay awake for more than an hour. It's frustrating."

"Your body obviously needs it."

I glance out of the window, suddenly realising I don't have a clue where we are. The street is residential, with large, detached properties set back from the road. Every garden is immaculate, and every driveway has a car on it that probably costs more than I made in a year at my office job.

"Where are we?"

Matt gives my brother a secret smile before he shrugs and opens the car door.

I glance at Aaron, my eyes narrowing. "What's going on?"

"Don't know," he lies.

I frown and climb out of the car. Matt holds a hand out to me, which I take without hesitation. The three of us walk towards the nearest property. It's huge. Stunning. It's red brick with large bay windows on the front and a detached double garage to the side. He walks up to the front door, and I'm starting to feel a little uncertain.

Until he pulls a set of keys from his pocket and pushes one into the lock. "Why do you have keys to this house?"

"Our house, babe. Mine and yours."

I stare at him. "You… you bought us a house?"

"You were dragging your heels so much about moving out of the flat."

"The flat will be more than ample space for us."

He kisses my head. "We need a garden, and room for our family to grow."

"Let's just get through baby number one before we talk about adding more," I joke, but the thought of a big family does appeal to me.

Matt pushes the front door open. "Go and look at your new home."

My brother grins at me. "Go on."

I step inside the hallway, my eyes everywhere. The decor is beautiful. Soft creams and greys. Classic. Modern. Clean.

There's a large living room, dining room, and a spare room that could be a playroom for the baby as he gets bigger. The kitchen is enormous, with an island in the middle of the room and a double oven. There's a seating area in there so we can eat in the kitchen or dining area.

The bedrooms are massive, two with ensuite. One for

us, one for Aaron—at least I assume so as the room is decorated to suit a teenager. There's a small room that could be used as guest room or study, a family bathroom, and then the last room.

As soon as Matt opens the door to it, I burst into tears. It's a nursery. Decorated in blues and greens, the room is soothing and warm. There's a cot against the wall and a large armchair that I can use to feed him in. "Did you… did you do this?"

"Yeah. Aaron helped. The baby will be in our room for a few months, but once he's old enough, he can move into here."

My brother beams at me. "Do you like it? I helped paint and put the furniture together."

"It's perfect," I say, choking on my words. "How long have you been doing this for?"

"We've had the keys for a month," Matt admits. "We can move in as soon as you want."

I close my eyes. This is a dream, a surreal dream in which all my wishes and hopes have been realised.

"Elyse, you okay?"

"I'm better than okay."

I kiss him.

"PDA. I'm out," Aaron mutters, leaving the room.

I laugh and kiss Matt again. "Thank you."

"For what?"

"Giving us a life we could never have envisaged."

"You deserve it, and more."

He wraps his arm around my shoulders, his eyes

crawling around the room. “Better hope that doc was right and that the kid is a boy.”

“I don’t think the colour matters.”

He kisses me. “I can’t wait to make my life with you.”

I can’t wait for that either. I love him, with everything I have and more.

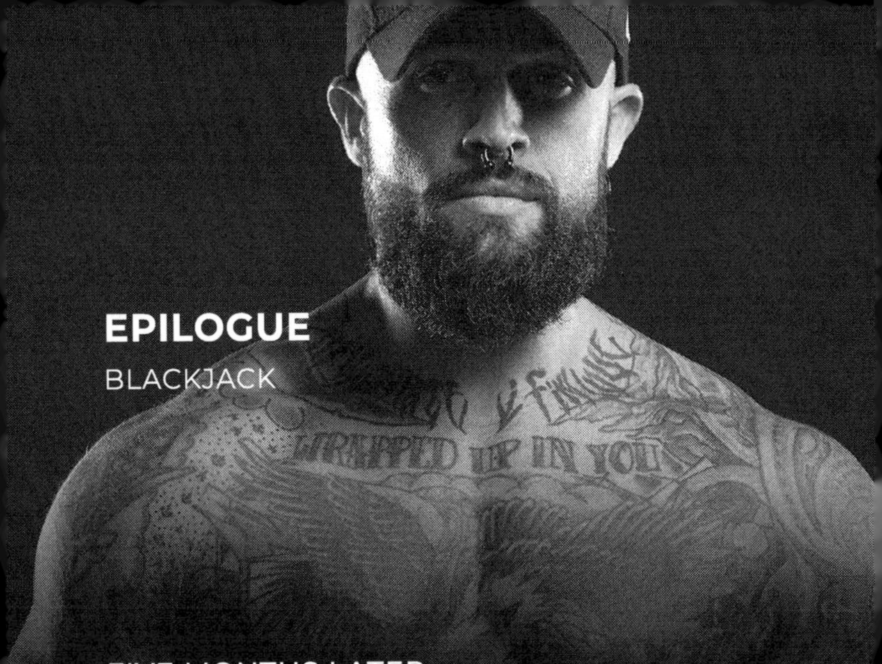

EPILOGUE

BLACKJACK

FIVE MONTHS LATER...

The darkness of the bedroom should be perfect for me to sleep, but for some reason I'm wide a-fucking-wake. It must be two or three am—I don't want to check the time on my phone in case it wakes Elyse up. She's been struggling to sleep lately too.

This pregnancy has been hard on her body.

I nuzzle into Elyse's back, my hand resting on swell of her large stomach. My son moves beneath my hand, and I feel reassured by that. I don't know how the fuck she's sleeping through his kicks and movements. I nuzzle against her back, trying to close my eyes and sleep.

Nothing.

Fuck. I don't want to get up and risk waking her, so I turn on my back, peering up the dark ceiling, listening to her deep and even breaths. In a matter of days, we could be holding our son. It's a weird feeling, but I'm not scared. I'm excited by the prospect.

Elyse's pregnancy has been relatively straight forward. The docs kept a close eye on her because of her blood pressure issue early on, but that didn't give her any issues throughout.

We've been lucky.

Every swell of her stomach as the months passed made me feel choked. Knowing she's carrying my baby makes me feel closer to her in a way I can't explain. We made something that's ours—both of ours. Something that ties us together for the rest of our lives.

I start to feel relaxed listening to her breaths, and my eyes feel heavy. I'm on the verge of going off when I hear a soft, "Matt..."

Her voice in the silence has my eyes popping open. "You okay?"

"I'm wet."

I chuckle. "Babe, it's the middle of the night. You're exhausted. You know I'll fuck you whenever you ask it but—"

"No, not that kind of wet." She grouches.

As she says it, I feel something damp against my leg. I lean over and switch the lamp on, before I peel back the covers. The sheet beneath us is soaked. My first thought is she peed herself.

"I think my waters broke," she whispers, and I see the fear in her eyes.

Shit. "Okay. Let's, uh, get you up and clean. Are you having contractions?"

"I think so. I don't know. I've been having pain since we went to bed."

My eyes flare. "You didn't think to mention that?"

"I thought it was Braxton-hicks!"

I try to calm myself. It doesn't matter right now. What matters is getting her to the hospital.

I get out of bed and come around to her side. I help her sit on the edge of the bed. Her leggings are black, but I can see they're damp around her crotch.

As if she's a kid, I peel them down her legs and toss them in the corner. "We have a laundry hamper," she grumbles.

"I couldn't give a fuck about that right now."

Wrapping an arm around her back, I help her to stand and walk her towards the ensuite. We get halfway across the room before she stops, panting and bending over. Her hand presses against her stomach. "Fuck, ouch."

She breathes through her nose as I rub her back, muttering soothing things and feeling fucking useless.

"Contraction?"

"Yeah. That felt stronger than the others."

"Okay. Let's get in the shower quick."

I help her into the cubicle and help her wash. It's not easy with her baby bump in the way, and she has a contraction in the middle of it all, but I wash her legs and feet, her pussy too, and then pull her out to dry her in the bedroom. Wrapped in a towel, I use another to pat her legs and feet before helping her get into clean underwear and a pair of leggings. We forgo a bra, and I pull one of my hoodies over her head. It clings to her bump as I tug it down.

"We need the overnight bag," she says. "And someone needs to sit with Aaron."

Her brother is thirteen now and could probably stay on his own, but I dial Mara anyway. She picks up after the fourth ring, sounding sleepy.

"Elyse is in labour," I say before she can get a word in.

She switches into doctor mode instantly. "How far apart are the contractions?"

I glance at Elyse, who has her eyes closed, her shoulders hunched over as she grips her stomach. "Pretty close. We need someone to stay with Aaron."

"Head to the hospital. I'll be there in ten minutes."

"Thanks, Mara."

"Oh, and Blackjack?"

"Yeah?"

"Congratulations."

"Thanks." I ignore how choked up I sound as I hang up. Quickly, I pull on a pair of joggers and a sweater before I carefully help Elyse to her feet.

She digs her nails into my arm, and I wince from the pain. I know it's not close to what she's feeling so I don't say anything, but I'm grateful when she loosens her grip.

"Oh, fuck. That hurts." She sounds breathless.

"Come on, let's get to the car."

"Good idea," she says. "The hospital has drugs."

I laugh, which is not a good idea because she glares at me. "You think it's funny I have to push a baby out of my vagina? Especially considering his father is a giant with a fat head?"

I huff out a breath as I try to keep her moving down the stairs. "I don't have a fat head."

"Your head is huge. I'm going to tear. There's no way I can birth a baby with your genes and not." She grabs my tee. "Don't let them cut me."

"Babe, just take a breath."

"What's all the noise?" Aaron's sleepy voice sounds from the landing. I glance up from the stairs. We've made it around halfway down.

"Your sister's in labour," I say.

"And it's his fault," she adds, wailing as another contraction hits. "Fucking fuckity shit!"

Aaron's eyes widen. "Do you, uh... need any help?"

"Mara's coming over. Just... don't burn the house down before she arrives."

"Noted. Elyse?" She glances up. "Good luck."

She mutters something under her breath, and I shift my shoulders before going back to helping her down the stairs.

It takes a while to get her out to the car, but once she's strapped in, I rush back into the house, get the hospital bag, and pull on a pair of running shoes I left by the front door.

Before I head out to the car, I pause in the hallway and sag against the wall. Fuck. This is happening.

I smile and laugh as I push off the wall, knowing in a few short hours I'll be a dad.

I take a breath, and then I drive my old lady to the hospital.

"He's so perfect," Pia coos as she holds on to my son's finger.

He is perfect. He has a layer of dark red hair on his head that matches my old lady's colouring, and he's wrapped in a soft grey blanket Mara and Trick bought us before the birth. His little fists swat at the air as his red puffy face wrinkles and smooths out, as if he's thinking of crying.

Elyse stares down at the baby in her arms, her eyes filled with so much love I feel like she might burst. "I love him so much," she admits.

I sink back in the chair at the side of the bed, my heart full too. He was six pounds four ounces, despite Elyse's concern about my fat head. He's tiny.

Mara leans in closer for a look. "Don't get me broody. I don't have time for a baby right now."

Elyse strokes our son's cheek. "There's no feeling better than this."

Valentina smiles. "That feeling never goes away."

"Do you guys have a name picked out yet?" Pia asks, smiling at her mother.

Elyse glances at me and then says, "Max."

Aaron says, "They wouldn't call him any of the names I picked."

"That's because you wanted shit like Tiberius," Elyse says.

"Yeah, instead you got Maximus."

"You are not calling my son Maximus."

Through the window of the room, I spot a few of my brothers. I push to my feet. "I'll be back in a moment," I tell Elyse, kissing her, then the top of my son's head.

The protective urges that wash through me are indescribable. I want to keep them both safe, and I would give my life to do it.

I step out into the corridor with a glance back at them. My whole world is in this room and leaving feels harder than it should.

I force myself to shut the door behind me and make my way to my brothers. Howler, Terror, Brew, Socket and Trick are filling the corridor and earning glares from the nursing staff.

"How's the kid?" Brew asks.

"Good. Healthy. He's got a set of lungs on him." He does.

"Congrats, man," Trick says with a grin.

I shake my head. "It still doesn't feel real." I scrub a hand over my beard.

Howler grins. "It's amazing, brother. You and Elyse did good."

"She did it all. She was a warrior in there."

She was. I saw shit I never want to talk about again in that room, and she did shit a human shouldn't be capable of.

"I need some fresh air," I say, glancing back at the room.

"I'll stay with them," Howler promises. "Go and get some air, take a breather."

I want to get Elyse flowers too. She fucking deserves more after what she did, but I don't think the hospital gift shop stocks enough things to show her my appreciation.

Terror comes with me, walking through the maternity ward and out into the front entrance of the hospital. We go to a bench and sink onto it. The cool air is soothing and helps clear my head of all the craziness that's happened since our child was born.

"Feel like the luckiest bastard on the planet," I admit.

"Hold on to that feeling, brother."

I intend to.

I'm a father.

Elyse gave me that gift, and I can never repay it.

If she hadn't been in the casino that day, if she hadn't slept with me and stolen my money, we wouldn't be here today, my son in her arms.

My life is complete, and that's because of Elyse Taylor.

Two weeks later…

Terror

I fucking hate collecting dues. It's the worst part of all the shit we have to do for the club. Give me a fucker to torture over beating up business owners for protection money. There's no sport in it.

I'm with Socket today.

The brother is grouchy as fuck. I don't know if married life isn't the bliss he intended, but he's driving me crazy moaning.

I zone him out as we head into Entice, a strip club in the centre of the city. I hate this place. It's dirty, seedy as fuck, and the girls on stage always look doped out of their brains.

Still, it's not my job to regulate this shit. We collect the money, we protect the club from outsiders, and we move on.

Despite being barely the afternoon, the lights are low, and the stage lit up. Two blondes are circling the poles in skyscraper high heels and thongs that barely cover their arses. Both girls are topless, their tits hanging out. Neither set are real.

I turn to watch Socket as he collects the money from Zack, the owner, before my eyes drift back to the stage. A new girl is climbing the steps to take over from one of the blondes. She wobbles on her heels and her eyes are heavy, even beneath the thick eyeliner. Her dark hair is long and curls down her back. She's not wearing a top either, just a thong that barely covers her cunt, and a phoenix tattoo runs down her hip.

A tattoo I'm intimately fucking acquainted with.

I don't say a word to Socket as I move towards the stage, my anger growing with every step. I don't know why I didn't recognise her at first. The hair isn't hers. I don't think so anyway. Last time I saw her, she had blonde hair cut to her shoulders.

Fuck, it is her.

The security arsehole tries to stop me from going up the steps. I pull back my fist and slam it into his face. He staggers back, and I continue on my path. Her eyes have come to me, seeing the commotion, and I know the exact moment she recognises me.

Her eyes flare and she steps back, trying to put some distance between us. There's no way in hell she can though. I'm close enough to grab her. I snag her wrist and tug her towards me. I notice instantly beneath the thick makeup that her eye is bruised, which is probably why she's slapped it on.

"The fuck are you doing?" I hiss at her.

Her chest heaves, making me hyper aware of the fact her tits are on display to everyone in the room. She lifts her chin, finding steel in her backbone suddenly.

"Are you trying to get me fired, Kayden?"

I growl at her, grabbing her arm and dragging her towards the stairs. Socket is waiting at the bottom, his hand pressed against the bouncer's throat to stop him attacking me.

"Kayden, stop!" she yells, dragging free from me. "You don't get to walk into my life and snarl at me. I'm not yours anymore."

I get in her face. "Wrong."

She shoves me, and I go back on a foot. "You're such a dick."

She rushes down the steps so fast I'm scared she's

going to break her ankle, but she is clearly used to wearing those heels, which makes my jaw clench.

"The hell, Terror?" Zack demands, coming over and raising his arms in the air. "Why are you ruining my business?"

I get in his face, grabbing the front of his jacket and dragging him to me. "How long has she been working here?"

"What?"

"How fucking long has she been taking her clothes off in your shit hole bar?"

The fear in his eyes tells me he recognises I'm not playing here. "About six months."

"She doesn't fucking do it again. I find out you've let her, and I'll set fire to this place with you in it."

"Hang on, she's my best girl. You can't just demand I—"

I round on him.

"I'm hanging on by a thread right now," I warn.

He backs down instantly. Socket wanders over to me. "Someone you know?"

That's an understatement.

"My fucking stepsister," I mutter. "And I'll burn this entire building down before I let her shake her arse on stage for total strangers."

GET A FREE BOOK AND EXCLUSIVE CONTENT

Dear Reader,

Thank you so much for taking the time to read my book. One of my favourite parts of writing is connecting with you. From time to time, I send newsletters with the inside scoop on new releases, special offers and other bits of news relating to my books.

When you sign up, you'll get a free book.

Find out more here:

www.jessicaamesauthor.com/newsletter

Jessica x

ENJOYED THIS BOOK?

Reviews are a vital component in any authors arsenal. It enables us to gain more recognition by bringing the books to the attention of other readers.

If you've enjoyed this book, I would be grateful if you could spend five minutes leaving a review on the book's store page. You can jump right to the page by clicking below:
https://books2read.com/TerrorUSMC

ALSO BY JESSICA AMES

Have you read them all?

UNTAMED SONS MC SERIES

Infatuation

Ravage

Nox

Daimon

Until Amy (Until Series and Sons Crossover)

Levi

Titch

Fury

Bailey

Stoker

Cage

FRASER CRIME SYNDICATE

Fractured Vows

The Ties that Bind

A Forbidden Love

UNTAMED SONS MC MANCHESTER SERIES

Howler

Blackjack

Terror

IN THE ROYAL BASTARDS SERIES

Into the Flames

Out of the Fire

Into the Dark

IN THE LOST SAXONS SERIES

Snared Rider

Safe Rider

Secret Rider

Claimed Rider (A Lost Saxons Short Story)

Renewed Rider

Forbidden Rider

Christmas Rider (A Lost Saxons Short Story)

Flawed Rider

Fallen Rider

STANDALONE BOOKS

Match Me Perfect

Stranded Hearts

ABOUT THE AUTHOR

Jessica Ames lives in a small market town in the Midlands, England. She lives with her dog and when she's not writing, she's playing with crochet hooks.

For more updates join her readers group on Facebook:
www.facebook.com/groups/JessicaAmesClubhouse

Subscribe to her newsletter:
www.jessicaamesauthor.com

facebook.com/JessicaAmesAuthor
twitter.com/JessicaAmesAuth
instagram.com/jessicaamesauthor
goodreads.com/JessicaAmesAuthor
bookbub.com/profile/jessica-ames

Printed in Great Britain
by Amazon

83307272R00150